THE AFTERWORD

THE

AFTERWORD

MIKE BRYAN

PANTHEON BOOKS · NEW YORK

All rights reserved under International and Pan-American
Copyright Conventions. Published in the United States
by Pantheon Books, a division of Random House, Inc.,
New York, and simultaneously in Canada by Random
House of Canada Limited, Toronto.

Pantheon Books and colophon are registered trademarks
of Random House, Inc.

Library of Congress Cataloging-in-Publication Data

Bryan, Mike.
The afterword / Mike Bryan.
p. cm.
ISBN 0-375-42212-9
1. Fiction—Authorship—Fiction. 2. Second Advent—
Fiction. 3. Best-sellers—Fiction. 4. Novelists—Fiction.
I. Title

PS3602.R94 A36 2003
813'.54—dc21   2002030710

www.pantheonbooks.com
Book design by Archie Ferguson
Printed in the United States of America

FIRST EDITION

2 4 6 8 9 7 5 3 1

THE AFTERWORD

Chapter One

WELL, WHY NOT? When a first novel by a workaday journalist takes root on the best-seller lists, breaking three records on the *New York Times* fiction list alone,[*] shocking all concerned, and when readers are always asking about the secret life of this or that episode in the story, about the finer points of theology, about the back story for the whole thing (some saga of perseverance and redemption, surely),

---

[*] Most weeks total (179, one more than *The Robe*, a page-turner from the fifties about the early Christian era); most weeks as No. 1 (37, one more than *The Bridges of Madison County*); and shortest novel to make the list at all (only 31,697 words, 97 fewer than *Einstein's Dreams*).

and about what I "really believe," why not answer all the questions, once and for all, with what might turn out to be a rather lengthy afterword to this handsome new edition of *The Deity Next Door*?

Plus a lot has changed since the novel came out—not everything, as some people tried to believe, but a lot, including the cultural context for my story. The hardcover of *Deity* had been on the lists for over a year but was finally losing steam when, on September 11, our sudden angry interest in Islam must have spilled over into a more thoughtful consideration of all the major religions; implicitly, I guess, my little confection about a new deity addresses some issues regarding the older ones. In any event, I can't deny that sales spiked sharply in the following months, and I started fielding a whole new set of questions.

Finally, I'm happy to perform this service to the trade because I haven't been doing anything else anyway. Along with everyone else, I did issue a couple of op-ed fatwas after the attacks, but otherwise I haven't been able to bestir myself to produce more journalism, of which we have plenty as it is. Nor am I a story-teller per se. This one idea has turned out great, but in all likelihood *Deity* will be the only novel from me—and just as well, because most of the worthwhile books from now on, ones that might hang on for a generation or even two, will be written either by amateurs, in effect, like Robert Pirsig (*Motorcycle Maintenance*), or by scribes who know how to chest their cards, like Jerome David Salinger. That's my theory. Our language is no longer fresh enough, nor does our culture care enough, to nurture and sustain for the long haul the imagination of any but the best. If I'm not among the best, if I don't feel that if I'm not typing I'm not living—and I don't—why in the world would I climb on this treadmill? Why write any but a book that's at least potentially new reading?

"Money!" is one answer I hear, and I stand

rebuked for my presumption. How well I remember, how soon I forget! Still, in an ideal world the aspiring novelist would give it one shot, then maybe a second, just conceivably a third; after that, unless you've demonstrated a genuine voice and vision (Cormac McCarthy), give it a rest. So lightning isn't likely to strike me a second time, and it did so the first time—getting down to business now—only because various other editorial projects were in various stages of falling through. In the year before I wrote *Deity* I failed to sell proposals for five books of nonfiction: *America Emeritus,* a diatribe against higher education (grade inflation, online course work, adjunct "professors," etc.); *"Obviously A Major Malfunction,"* an exposé of the NASA bureaucracy as emblematic of all bureaucracies; *Dead End: The Last Road Book,* an indictment of mass-market interstate culture; *Drive-by Journalism Goes on Vacation,* in which I join the natives at Yellowstone, Yosemite, and the Grand Canyon in the middle of August;

and *All Those Michaels and Me, Just Plain Mike,* a wide-ranging condemnation of this celebrity culture of ours. (Regarding that last title, I had in mind Michaels Jackson, Jordan, Eisner, Crichton, Milken, Douglas, and Dukakis. I have to admit, one reason I've always had a soft spot for a certain former heavyweight champ, while conceding his feral nature, is that I've never, ever seen a reference to Michael Tyson, and you can imagine my dismay when one of the early marketing people for *Deity* wondered aloud, in my presence, whether Michael Bryan wouldn't play better as the author's name on the cover.)

The editors who kept rejecting these ideas suggested that perhaps I was in a rut, and perhaps they had a point. Regardless, I thank them, because if I'd sold any one of those books I probably wouldn't have written this one, because each would have been a big book in its own right, surely—a facetious boast immediately contradicted by my depressing experience with *Shrinks: They Do the Talking, We Listen.* That was the one proposal I *had* sold a couple of years earlier, when oral histories still had a life, and I'd gotten off to a great start with the first guy I talked to, a psychiatrist I knew in Denver who told me that what it comes down to—almost quoting now—is sitting and listening to the folks, letting us say whatever we want to say about ourselves and how we feel, not giving us a hard time, helping us look at what we're doing and how we're feeling, helping us look at what's getting in the way of what we want to be doing and feeling, trying to help us set that aside, and, finally, scavenging for whatever seems relatively healthy and strong and trying to reinforce that.

What a sweet notion, and my friend buttressed it with a series of fascinating stories. I was excited. I thought this was going to be a great book, but from there it was downhill all the way. I'd never encountered such a set of guarded or simply uninteresting men and women as those psychologists and psychiatrists, and I didn't have either the patience or the travel budget to persevere. I should have paid more attention to another remark by my friend, who told me, "When I was a first-year resident I had this wonderful teacher who believed that people go into psychiatry in order to learn how to communicate, because they don't know how. There's truth in that. Absolutely." I also realized that the appeal of the powerful stuff in the interviews I did collect was primarily voyeuristic, that what the editor wanted was nothing more than some kind of legitimate-looking cover for printing yet more pathography (on a miniature, non-celebrity scale, but no less disreputable for that), just as the media's orgy of self-appraisal and perhaps even self-criticism after some heinous event always calls for showing the heinous event one more time, and just as I now cite one story from the psychiatrist already quoted as an example of the kinds of stories I'd have felt guilty about citing in *Shrinks: They Do the Talking, We Listen.*

"Some cases are just god-awful," my friend began in response to my question about his most god-awful cases. "The most noteworthy of those in my experience was this lady who was quite depressed and also an alcoholic. I think—this is some years ago now—that she was referred to me by another doctor who was seeing her husband, too, and he got in too deep with this really wild couple and so referred the woman to me for individual therapy. Couples therapy can get out of hand; you move from a two-body system to a three-body system, and the variables increase dramatically. Sometimes you need a co-therapist to pull you back when you get too involved in the family crisis, when you feel you're not in control and you think that some work with each person away from the spouse would be helpful.

"Anyhow, this lady got referred to me. She was in graduate school in economics, I believe it was, a lady in her thirties, very bright, second marriage, a couple of kids from the first marriage who were having problems, and *she* was having problems. There were lots of problems. Always something going on in that family. Always. This woman was one of those borderline personalities: people who have a problem with how they live their lives, but they are not crazy, they are not psychotic or neurotic in the sense of a specific, well-defined psychosis or neurosis. These are called personality disorders—a *style* of living that causes them problems. There are a bunch of different ones. And for every such person going to a therapist, there is one or more who is not in therapy. I don't doubt that for a minute.

"This lady did have some superficial trappings of health. She'd just finished her economics degree. That requires a certain amount of ego strength. But she had no idea what she was going to do with it. The notion of being an economist appealed to her, but the notion of going to work in the real world scared the hell out of her. Except for the couple of minutes after she got her diploma, graduating was not a positive experience for her. And that's often true with those experiences. It's like, well, am I somebody else now? No, I'm still the same person I always was. That can be real saddening. But she took it to an extreme. She *really* got depressed. Devastated.

"I was seeing her twice a week. This woman was very needy, very demanding, very draining. Lots of phone calls. With somebody like that you have to be pretty active in therapy, too. I feel that way. You can't just sit back and listen to them. She was too sick. You can only do that with healthy people, or relatively healthy people. There's a well-known story about an analyst who spent years trying to psychoanalyze schizophrenics. He wasn't getting anywhere. Schizophrenia is organic; analysis can't deal with that. He finally quit trying when he realized he wanted to kill all of them.

"Patients like this lady are too sick to tolerate real unstructured situations. The more you talk the more you structure the situation; you're letting someone know what you expect. If you adopt analytic silence, you're creating a situation without clear expectations, and that's real anxiety provoking. This lady didn't need any more anxiety.

"Soon enough, I felt things finally got beyond what could be handled on an outpatient basis, and I called a friend of mine who had access to a residential treatment facility. I was concerned this lady was suicidal, from what she was telling me about how she was functioning— vegetating, couldn't sleep, couldn't get out of bed, ruminating about killing herself. She had been on several different medications, none of which she had responded to particularly well. So I made the hospital arrangements and talked with her husband and then told her, 'Look, you need to do this and you need to stick with it. It's gonna be tough. You're going to want to leave.'

"Unbeknownst to me, she had extracted from her husband a promise that if she decided to leave the facility he would absolutely not make any effort to keep her there involuntarily. I didn't know about that deal. She was there a couple of weeks and things were starting to get a little rough and she decided she wanted to leave. I had one last call with her, strongly urging her to stay there, so much so that I told her that I would not see her in my office if she left, because that would imply that the sessions would have some sense, and they wouldn't. 'I'm not going to see you,' I said. I talked with her husband and told him it was a dumb promise he had made, that he should go ahead and commit her anyway. He wouldn't. She came home. A couple of weeks later she left town, turned up in a hotel somewhere, and took the overdose.

"Her husband called me with the news. Several things went through my head. I thought back on my decision not to see her and thought, well, maybe if I'd seen her she wouldn't have done that. I thought about the husband's decision not to commit her, and was pissed at him, real angry at him. The other reaction I had, well, she was just a real tough lady to deal with, and the knowledge that I would no longer have to—this brought me a certain amount of relief."

That last remark wipes me out every time. We're intensely focused on this woman's terrible pain, only to be suddenly confronted with this frank admission by her trusted physician. You have to know that this is a terrific guy, utterly devoted to his patients, and yet one of his reactions on hearing about the suicide is blessed, guilty relief. Wow. As you've undoubtedly realized, this story is the basis for the scene in the psychiatric hospital in *Deity*, but my point here is that the denouement is a brutal commentary on our essential, bottom-line egotism and selfishness. It's always all about me, for all of us, and this holds for religion and faith, too—religion and faith most of all, you could argue. (. . . *and God created man in His own image; in the image of God He created him:* that's a tad self-aggrandizing of us, isn't it?)

But *Shrinks* fell apart, so none of my book ideas were happening, and then—to conclude this litany of misadventures without which I'd never have written *Deity*—a series of ads I'd been writing for Federal Express for placement in the *Wall Street Journal* as a "Sports Journal" column about sports-related business topics finally became too much trouble. This column ran biweekly, every other Friday, and it wasn't long before every submission became a battle. They—someone at Federal Express, maybe several people, maybe a committee, perhaps the whole board—eyeballed every word and, as I eventually figured out, *counted* them. After a few months it became clear that my chief antagonist was an executive in Memphis who thought my sentences were too long. Too long for the *Wall Street Journal*?! I happened to know that the paper is—or was, at that time; I can't speak for today—written at the twelfth-grade level, a bit of inside information acquired from the quality-control editor at the *Dallas Morning News,* who'd told me about the rating standards when I called her with yet another error of usage in that family newspaper when we lived in that city some years ago.

(Even she acknowledged that this time I had a truly interesting "catch." The word in question appeared in a story about groundbreaking studies demonstrating that divorced women tend to cope with the situation better than their former husbands—cope emotionally, that is, not financially. Near the end, the author asserted that these women had come to view their marriages as a "vice." That description stopped me cold. I know there are unholy marriages—the one in *Rosemary's Baby* comes to mind—but, generally speaking, who looks back on a failed marriage as a vice? Nor did the idea fit with the rest of the piece, in which no one was arguing that the women harbored the feelings of guilt or shame associated with vice. What they'd felt was hampered, thwarted, trapped, etc. The byline indicated that the story had been pulled from the *New York Times* News Service, and, as my luck would have it, the national edition of the *Times,* to which we also subscribed, ran that story the same day. I immediately skimmed to the paragraph in question, where I was rewarded with one of the great *Eureka!* moments of my life: in this original version of the story, the word had been *vise*—v-i-s-e—which made perfect sense in the context: the women look back on the failed marriage as a vise. But perhaps I was making too much of this, so I conferred with my wife and the first few callers and e-mailers of the day, all of whom agreed that, yes, "vice" for "vise" was an exceptionally provocative miscue, probably the handiwork of some editorial slacker who took the word "vise" for a misspelling.)

In any event, it was during my discussion with the quality-control editor at the *Morning News* (a position since scuttled) that I learned about the twelfth-grade reading level for the *Wall Street Journal* (one grade higher than achieved by the *New York Times,* two higher than by *USA Today* and the *Morning News*), and it was this knowledge that triggered my indignation with the corporate cavil from FedEx about the length of my sentences. CEOs read the *Wall Street Journal,* COOs, CFOs, and I was being instructed that these titans of industry couldn't handle twenty-seven words— the longest sentence in any of the "Sports Journal" pieces, because I'd gone back and counted. Meanwhile, the first sentence of our Declaration of Independence has seventy-one words; of our Constitution, fifty-two; and the last sentence of the Gettysburg Address has eighty-two of them. Under the circumstances, I didn't think twenty-seven words were too many to ask for, but the battle for approval from Memphis got nasty. I begged for the occasional twenty-five, they wanted twenty, tops.

I was incensed, and as a change of pace, ostensibly, but also as a way to get fired and thereby get out of this onerous if well-paid gig, I commissioned my friend Roy N., a screenwriter out in L.A. with a genius for knockabout comedy, to come up with an offbeat "Sports Journal." Roy quickly produced a mailbag of bogus letters from the supposedly loyal readers of my popular column, accompanied by my witty rejoinders. The last one was from a guy who'd heard about these terrific columns on subjects touching sports and business that appeared every other Friday in the *Wall Street Journal,* but he'd acquired that newspaper every other Friday for just this purpose and could never find the column.

What gives? he queried, signed DQ.

No, no, I replied, you misunderstood: every *other* Friday.

Now, come on, that's pretty funny, and the sentences were plenty short, but the powers that be in Memphis must have read something into that letter that wasn't intended (possibly assuming that "DQ" stood for Dan Quayle) and rejected the submission. A few days later, I called the FedEx guy I was dealing with and suggested that "Sports Journal" was no longer worth the hassle to me, and he assured me that it was no longer worth it to him, either.

In my case, therefore, the story behind the best-selling novel turns out to be not so much about perseverance and redemption—not in the beginning, at least—and much more about the roll of the dice: if FedEx hadn't been so juvenile concerning the length of my sentences, I might still be writing those trivial columns. *Deity* turns out to be as contingent on the contrivances of—God? someone else? or just plain life?—as everything else. And so much for my deal with Roy N.: if by some chance FedEx had accepted his piece, we would've been straight on the matter of the $1,500 he owed me. That didn't work out, but Roy died recently, so now we're more than straight.

As it happened, just a couple of weeks after the conclusion of the FedEx/*Wall Street Journal* debacle I passed through Dallas and had lunch with a few friends from the Bible college where I'd kibitzed for a semester about a decade ago while working on a book about evangelicals.* (In retrospect—a retrospect that set in almost immediately, because the book didn't sell a lick—I realized that this well-intentioned endeavor had been fatally politically incorrect from both perspectives: for the secular market,

---

*Chapter and Verse: A Skeptic Revisits Christianity, Random House, 1991; Penguin, 1992; out of print, 1993.

which doubts whether it's possible to believe the Bible and chew gum at the same time, I'd given these Neanderthals in Texas the time of day; for the Christian market, I'd sincerely engaged them and their beliefs, but then had been so stubborn or obtuse as to walk away still unsaved.) Lunch was fun—my friends are smart, sophisticated folks, believe me, not Neanderthals—and a few days later, back at my post in New York City, I was surprised to find myself pondering yet again the whole subject of belief and doubt, because the basic problem never goes away. Any sort of doctrinaire Christianity is a dead letter to the secular world, it's true, but even Sartre told de Beauvoir late in their lives that he didn't see himself as just so many exquisitely organized cells, that he had a sense of himself as a being who was expected, prefigured, called forth by a creating hand—an image that willy-nilly referred him back to God.

Well, you reply, the revered old atheist was

just worn out by this point, with his clutch slipping badly, but what about the analogy he drew between our twentieth-century predicament and the man who enters a café to meet a friend? The protagonist looks around. The friend isn't there. The protagonist orders an espresso macchiato, lights up, waits. The friend doesn't show. The protagonist's presence in the café is now defined by the absence of the friend. This is the main fact of his situation, and whatever he does next—exhibit patience or get angry, wait a while longer or storm out the door—is a response to what isn't there.

To my mind, that nails the situation precisely. I happen to agree with my evangelical pals who argue that the irreligious world may not even be capable of sustaining the rest of us, who joke about the Christians with one bumper sticker—"Jesus Is Coming, Look Busy"—and about ourselves with another—"Life's a Bitch, Then You Die." Or, all joking aside, we wake up at four A.M. in a cold, clammy sweat with the thick, viscous blackness of a universe fifteen billion meaningless light-years in diameter suffocating (or sometimes drowning) the little that's left of our *not*-God-given spirits. What can I say? Do I have to defend myself? This business still intrigues me, and no sooner had I returned to New York than I was pondering a second stab at the challenges posed both to and *by* Christianity. Could I find some way to work this persistent problem a second time, preferably in some more successful way?

I guess an editorial trauma like the one I'd just endured with FedEx would turn anyone's thoughts to fiction, where they let you have longer sentences (and in the afterword as well: the second sentence here has 104 words, not counting the footnote, all handcrafted for the purpose of this admittedly peevish point), because half an hour after I sat down at my desk I was entertaining the idea of a novel about a new deity—not a delusional patient who mistakenly believes he's such a being, but a young man who really *is* divine. And not an apocalyptic Christian potboiler straight out of Revelation like the best-sellers by Tim Lahaye and J. B. Jenkins, nor the story of a quick, unauthorized visit by Jesus Christ, as in the "Grand Inquisitor" story in *The Brothers Karamazov,* nor a gothic tale about paranormal powers, nor a spoof of some sort, but a real book for readers inclined more to thinking than to either believing or disdaining—or, at the least, readers willing to leaven their belief or their disdain with some thinking.

A new messiah: how does our secular, more or less post-Christian popular culture handle this little problem?! I sacrilegiously pictured the leering Jack Nicholson smashing through the door in *The Shining* while screaming, "I'm back!" And how does this new deity understand his incredible situation, come to terms with it, and figure out his next move—all of which posed some difficulties for the Rabbi of Nazareth two thousand years ago, in a time when basic religious faith of one sort or another was simply in the air and, like the oxygen itself, inhaled without pause for deliberation. Wouldn't the job be doubly difficult for any messiah today, when conditions have changed?

I liked it. I liked it a lot. I'm not a storyteller by instinct, and I have no talent for spinning out an intricate plot for its own sake, but this idea intrigued me precisely because it didn't seem to be for its own sake. The Bible may be yesterday's book for many people, but shifting the scene of the encounter from ancient Palestine to Manhattan or some other modern Gomorrah could invite us to think afresh about the whole idea of divinity and faith. Such was my early chutzpah. And although I mention Palestine and, by implication, the religions based there, initially I was thinking of a deity only in the most general terms. I wasn't thinking about whether my man would turn out to be the long-awaited messiah of the Jewish tradition, or a new and unexpected divinity in the

Christian tradition, or perhaps even the first incarnation in a new tradition. He wasn't going to be a Muslim or yet another divine figure in the Hindu pantheon, but beyond this I just didn't know or particularly care. (How many times have I been asked if the "he" was a given from the beginning? Dozens, and I've admitted every time that a goddess simply never occurred to me. I wish she had. That would have been really interesting.)

Jotting my early notes, I assumed that I, or anyone, would be virtually incapable of telling such a story straight today. Frankly, irony is what I expected to deploy in my narrative, and how could I possibly proceed without some kind of diversionary angle or narrative framing device (as I later learned such devices are called)? I shopped around for possibilities, but the shelves were empty. I couldn't find or think up a single trick, and after a week I decided I couldn't find anything because that wasn't the way to go with the story. Should it ever happen again, the coming of a new deity will be no joke, it will be serious business, and I'd have to treat it as such in my novel. (Already a big hit, *Deity* may also have benefited from the proscription on irony in the arts and letters notoriously decreed by some big-time national magazine editor immediately after the attack on the Twin Towers, because the novel isn't ironic in the least—benefited for a week or so, at least, because that's about how long the pro-scription remained in effect.) *Deity* is now often referred to as a fable, which is fine with me, nor do I object when someone cares to say that it has the qualities of a gospel. When I'm confronted by my lack of standing to write any-thing for which that designation might be appropriate, as I have been more than once, I ask acerbically, Whose new gospel would have more credence for you, mine or Jerry Falwell's? That usually works.

With this basic decision about tone now in hand, I turned to what I knew was the next important question: a name. As it happens, "Blaine" turns out to be an unpopular name for Blaine, and I had an idea this would be the case, because, almost to a man or woman, friends who critiqued early drafts of the story didn't like the name at all and proposed one or more alternatives. Their opposition surprised me, because I don't think I've ever quarreled with any novelist about the names of the characters. I don't think the names are that important, except with Dickens and Wodehouse, and I don't think we generally care, but maybe it's different if the character is divine. Faced with that firestorm of early opposition, I did agree to reconsider all the alternatives, but I still couldn't accept Matthew, John, Paul, Peter, Mark, Joshua, David, and so on. Just too obvious. For a second time I rejected all the multi-syllabic names that are so popular now—Nathaniel, Alexander, Christopher, Brandon, and the rest—and the single syllables like Max and Guy that seem designed to challenge the polysyllables in some semiotic way. Shaquille, Evander, Latrell, Enrique, Mariano, and the like were also still out, because I knew the story would be complicated enough to figure out with an Anglo messiah.

No, I insisted on a simple, modern, generic, Waspish name with no biblical connotations and minimal cultural aspirations, a name that would implicitly establish both the secular cultural setting and the irony of the new situation: yes, times have changed, but now they may have to change again, because now we have this uninvited new deity. (I told the story straight, but I couldn't do anything about the irony at the heart of it.) After considerable discussion and a couple of actual arguments, I stayed with "Blaine" on the grounds that a name that grated on so many readers might be a *good* sign. Maybe your distaste means that you care about this deity and his fate; maybe you even care a little more because you don't like his name. (When the book finally fell to No. 2 on the *Times* list, one friend with whom I'd had this argument quipped, "According to your logic, you'd still be No. 1 if you'd gone with Sylvester.")

Blaine he is, but now what? What about his family? Where was he born? He's definitely not a carpenter, but what's his situation otherwise? If I'm establishing the modern cultural context, surely I need some kind of modern family for him; maybe his parents figure in the divorce statistics. Maybe they do, but on these questions the ideas failed to flow, very likely because the questions just didn't interest me, because they almost never do. I'm reading along in a novel, having a good time, sucked in by the story, and all of a sudden I'm supposed to care about what happened between the guy and his father twenty years ago? I say a writer is doing well to establish a few main characters who strike us as real people. By bringing in family backgrounds with extended expository passages, you're probably stretching your vision and talent beyond the breaking point. I know I would be. My best proof here is Hemingway. What do we know about the early years of his characters? Essentially nothing, but start adding a few such paterfamilias paragraphs to *The Sun Also Rises* and see what happens to the air in that balloon. And he's Hemingway! For the life of me I don't understand why so many lesser writers fail to heed the lesson and thereby fall into error. Besides, from the Bible we don't learn much of Jesus's own background and early life—and from the Gospels of Mark and John, nothing at all. These two authors dispense with the Annunciation, virgin birth, adoration, and advancement of the baby Jesus as presented in Matthew and Luke, and this is one reason Mark and John are the more powerful stories, in my opinion.

In *The Deity Next Door,* therefore, the little

you do learn about Blaine's parents, his brother and two sisters, life around the house, early schooling, boyhood pals, adolescent angst, disastrous first date, college-admission anxiety—all of it, the works—is in the briefest passing. Some readers are surprised to realize, when I point out the fact during bookstore readings, that I haven't even provided Blaine with a last name. But do you miss any of this information? I don't think so. The silence on these subjects was the best way I could come up with to imply that this particular deity comes from no particularly religious background: no Annunciation, virgin birth, adoration, or escape into Mexico in the arms of his father; no early advancement beyond the norm in any respect. If some modern-day magi—astronomers at the local university, perhaps—had followed an exceptionally bright and timely comet to the delivery room, don't you think I'd have told you?

In *The Last Temptation of Christ,* Nikos Kazantzakis brought his story of Jesus up to date
in its thematic emphases while retaining the
setting in the ancient world, which made me
realize that I'd have to be even more radical
by way of updating, because Blaine grew up
with Ronald Reagan and a Madonna of a different sort. Whatever his background and his
future—Jewish, Christian, or hybrid—we know
one thing: he isn't the descendant of desert
tribesmen who've spent too many years baking
beneath the glaring sun, besotted with their
perhaps unique monotheism. This just can't be
happening to Blaine, a man with no marked
commitment to what is, by now, a tradition getting a little long in the tooth at the end of its
second millennium—but it *is* happening—but
how can this possibly be? So cut immediately
to the first chase: the ambivalence and confu-

sion any deity or messiah in the West would feel today. I wanted to plant the seeds of divine conviction-*cum*-perplexity in Blaine's mind as soon as possible.

With Jesus, the conviction part had been easy for the Gospel authors: in Matthew and Luke, the announcement of his greatness preceded his birth; in Mark and John, John the Baptist serves this purpose. I had neither option. I had to come up with something else that would give Blaine the nascent idea. In this world, lacking as it does the cultural context of widespread belief—not rote observance and religiosity, not what people tell pollsters, but honest-to-goodness inhaled belief—the new deity has to have *his own* conversion experience, in effect, and my first stab at such an experience for Blaine—just to give you an idea how I (and real novelists, probably) hunt for ideas—was a scene at a Mets game to which Blaine has taken his son one evening. (That fatherhood fact came out that way as I was writing along: just like that, Blaine has a son, and months later I decided, after much deliberation, to stick with it. This new deity, perhaps this new messiah of ours, is a father. So what? It's not exactly a Catholic turn of events, I'll admit, but it's possible: most Protestant denominations more or less require a wife and family for their preachers, because better the scandals of adultery and divorce and remarriage to the younger woman than those of—but never mind. If some readers unilaterally assume at this early point in the tale that Blaine is a Protestant deity, I'm not going to argue.)

I decided that Blaine's son *should* have a biblical or biblical-sounding name, and I chose Timothy, and in the fifth inning of this game at Shea the batter lifts a high pop fly over the infield, and—to make a surprisingly long scene short—that ball never comes down, and the reason it doesn't is that Blaine, on the spur of the moment, transposes it (I can't think of a better word to describe what happens) into

Tim's jacket pocket. On the field, however, no one knows this, because Blaine substitutes a new ball into play in midair. Then I thought about having the ball disappear, period, with clever headlines in the next day's tabloids ("Going . . . going . . . gone—for good!"), but all this seemed to serve my own enjoyment of baseball more than the story I was developing. It was too banal, or silly, or something, so I dumped it.

Blaine and his family live in an apartment building in New York because I lived in an apartment building in the city when I wrote *The Deity Next Door*. (I also liked the surprise here, because most people, when pressed on the matter (as they are, implicitly, when they're reading the novel), probably don't picture the new deity living in an apartment building somewhere.) Blaine's apartment remains unidentified, but it's remarkably similar in many details to our place at the time, London Terrace on West Twenty-fourth Street in Chelsea, between Ninth and Tenth Avenues, where we moved solely because of the swimming pool in the basement, one of the few such pools in the whole city, and the only one in a building we could possibly afford. I knew I could take advantage of the almost automatic association, in a story about divinity, between swimming *in* water and walking *on* water, so I tried such a scene now, copying the fact that the pool at London Terrace is adjacent to the health club, that you have to circle a balcony above it in order to reach the club, and that the placid water glows with a luscious, unearthly light on Wednesdays, when the ceiling lights are turned off because the pool is closed. Blaine can't swim worth a damn, but he does work out with the light weights in the health club. What if he's looking down from the balcony above the pool one Wednesday afternoon on the way to his workout and says to himself, somewhat illogically but with a sudden insight analogous to the one at the ball game, I might not be able to swim those twenty-five yards, but I'll bet I could walk them? He goes downstairs to the locker room, which is on the same level as the pool, opens the gate, steps onto the deck, checks the balcony to make sure no one is coming, and gingerly steps forth onto the surface of this small chlorinated sea.

Workable, I thought, but premature, so I saved it for later. Then I had the brainstorm that would serve me well over the next twelve months: I consulted the Christian Gospels for guidance. In Matthew, the first miracle is when Jesus heals every kind of disease and sickness among the people; in both Mark and Luke, his first miracle is the exorcism of the unclean spirit from one of the hecklers. Now, John's first miracle is different—the lovely story in which Jesus turns the water into wine for the wedding party in Cana—but three out of four for healing convinced me to follow this lead by upping the ante right at the beginning of Blaine's career with a miraculous cure—and not just any such cure, but a special one, because the real audience at this point isn't the local populace, as with Jesus's healings, but rather Blaine himself. Remember, he hasn't been announced or promoted in any way. In the first pages of *Deity* we've seen him only as a nice man, a reliable breadwinner, a dutiful husband, a doting father, Mets fan, left-handed Aquarius, somewhat superstitious, careful to get out of bed on the same side that he got in on—this kind of thing. *He has no idea* about his divinity and has to be jolted into the first stage of understanding. To this end, he will cure young Timothy of cancer.

I want to acknowledge that the specific idea of leading up to this first miracle by way of the minutely described life cycle of a cancer cell was given to me, unwittingly, by my friend Steve S., a writer in New Jersey who used an equivalent strategy in a thriller he wrote about biological warfare. In that book, Steve describes his virion in such cunning detail he could be accused of anthropomorphizing them. My two pages are a pale imitation of that tour de force but still effective enough, I think, as they implicitly set up the world we live in: one of vast knowledge and professional science, not one of demons cast out by a holy man, or even by a deity. Such exorcism scenes from Jesus's career, especially the one in which he cures the Gadarene demoniac by casting the demons (at their own request) into a herd of swine, with the beasts then rushing pell-mell down a steep bank into the Sea of Galilee—such a scene[*] tells the doubting modern mind just about all it needs to know about the Bible. At the same time, however, our science, though it may know about the cancer cells, cannot, in many cases, cope with them. If his son is to live, Blaine must accomplish the feat himself. Cancer cells are real, demons aren't, but sometimes the only cure for each is the same: a miracle.

---

[*]Matthew 8:28–34; Mark 5:1–20; Luke 8:26–39.

If Blaine has a son, the boy has to have a mother as well, a fact of life that didn't occur to me until I'd been working on the hospital scene for days, and then I thought, well, so be it, the possibly Protestant next messiah is married and let his wife's name be Melanie. What does Blaine tell Melanie about the sudden remission of their son's cancer? That was an easy call: he says nothing, because he isn't sure what happened and doesn't trust the most obvious explanation. How could he possibly have had any part at all in this apparently miraculous cure? It's absurd. Moreover, is this business of possibly being a deity something he's going to tell his wife first? I polled my friends, and, with a couple of exceptions, they agreed that he wouldn't. My own wife more than agreed, assuring me that she wouldn't want to know about my divinity, period. So for the time being Melanie remained on or near the sidelines.

Or was it even a real miracle? Blaine knows he has played a role here—Tim's was no spontaneous remission of a secular sort—but perhaps God has simply answered his prayer, even though Blaine never really prayed. I wanted Blaine to intuit, if nothing more, that something more active than prayer has been involved—something, but exactly what he doesn't know. His early answers must be provisional—but only for him, not for us. Going into this scene, we have to *know* he's a deity—not some kind of science fiction superman possessed of strange powers, not some character who's been touched by an angel, not an angel itself, but something more.

Okay, how do I draw this distinction, given that modern readers—even modern Christian readers—have been trained to think in exactly the opposite terms? How do I manipulate you into accepting without question Blaine's divinity even as Blaine himself struggles with his own early understanding? Again, let the Bible lead the way. Matthew's and Luke's stories of the Annunciation and the Adoration, to take two examples, don't prove a thing without the accompanying blunt declaration that they *are* the Annunciation and the Adoration. The claim is presented as the fact. Mark and John are even more direct when they brazenly identify Jesus Christ with God in their respective first verses. That's the only way to do it, really—by fiat—and I needed an equivalent unequivocal directness and simplicity with which to establish both Blaine's divinity and, initially, his total ignorance of this divinity, so I scrolled all the way back to the beginning of the story and laid the groundwork by adding the final clause to the first sentence: ". . . and he has no idea that he's divine."

A few readers have complained that they don't like the way this gives away the story so early, but they're simply wrong. They don't understand that without some such declaration, we don't have a story at all. We have to know that Blaine is not in the position of the devout nuns in Ron Hansen's *Mariette in*

Ecstasy and Mark Salzman's *Lying Awake,* two recent novels in which we're led (with exquisite skill in each case) to question the exact nature of the protagonists' stigmata and visions, respectively. From the beginning, I knew that *The Deity Next Door* would work only if the stakes were higher than in those two stories; only if we're encountering actual divinity, not mere holiness or saintliness or paranormality; only if there's no question of such explanations as the brain tumor that afflicts Sister John of the Cross in Salzman's novel; only if the question is not "What is Blaine?" but "What's he going to do with his divinity?"

Chapter Two[*]

INITIALLY, Frank Harris was a Methodist minister, because Blaine might be a Protestant deity, as indicated by his marriage and his son, but wouldn't it be witty to have Blaine decide that something this serious deserves and might even require a Catholic cleric whose institutional roots go all the way back to the founding? That's what I decided. (Couldn't Blaine be Jewish and consult a rabbi? Sure he could be Jewish, and maybe he should be, and maybe he should consult a rabbi, and maybe I would have

---

[*]An afterword with chapters—probably another publishing first.

sold even more books, because Jews buy 40 percent of all the books sold in this country, an independent bookseller told me (40 percent of the real books, maybe she meant, not the others as well), but now we're talking about a whole different novel, as things have turned out. I hadn't worried in the beginning about which tradition, if any, Blaine would eventually take his place in, but by this point that decision is pretty much out of my hands. Novelists will tell you that all kinds of decisions are made for them by forces unknown, and so it was with *The Deity Next Door.* In my mind, and I believe in the mind of the reader, it's now clear that Blaine is a deity who will work out his destiny within the Christian tradition.)

Of course, Protestants vigorously disagree with the implicit suggestion that Blaine has to consult a priest because somehow the Catholic faith is the more authentic one. They've always argued just the opposite, that theirs is the genuinely serious faith, the one that demands real discipline and passion for Christ, that the Catholic faith is too old for its own good, degenerating as it has into rote observance enforced by a self-serving bureaucracy that—but never mind again. In Dallas, it was a real treat for me to hear Bible-thumping preachers declaim on the subject of the professional paid religionists who run the Roman wing of Christianity, as if these Protestant preachers of the good book aren't professional and paid themselves (and, in the bigger churches, paid much more than the pontiff, I'm sure, not counting those incomparable papal perks). They warn the unwary that the whole point of the sacramental denominations (plural, to include Eastern Orthodoxy) is to drug their adherents with incense and strange incantations and to insulate them from any demands of the faith. Beware the Sunday-morning faith that may get you through the week but not into heaven! So it's easy to find conservative Protestants who'll tell you bluntly that they doubt the saved status of a Catholic: to hell with Church tradition, literally, if that's all you've got going for you. Likewise, there must be Catholics who don't give anyone from outside their church much of a chance.

(If you want my opinion in one paragraph, a large part of the problem between the two main wings of Christianity is simply the audacity of the basic claim that an itinerant Jew born in a crude manger two thousand years ago and subsequently crucified on a Roman cross for his heretical message and truculent behavior is God Incarnate, the key to the truth of the cosmos. This revolutionary is the only redemption recognized by God for our original sin in the Garden of Eden? Swear allegiance to this incredible story or suffer the consequences for all eternity? Even by the standards of Jesus's time—pagan and Jewish—these were bold propositions, rejected by all but a handful of the residents of Palestine. Viewed dispassionately in our culture today—well, can you name a more radical set of ideas in the history of Western civilization? Those who've left the churches altogether are quite certain that whatever's going on in the cosmos, this can't possibly be it, case closed, grow up. Among those who do believe this Christian story, or try to, or even just pretend to, it's easy to understand how they might either take refuge in the auspices of the Catholic Church, which has already done much of the work of believing for them, or swing in the opposite direction and bask in the sheer audacity of going it alone with their unmediated Protestant faith. It's also easy to see how such divergent volitions would struggle to find common ground.)

Importuned in my mind by Protestant pleas, I nevertheless decided to go with the Catholic priest in my novel about the new deity, and now I think the choice was close to necessary. I prove this by inviting you to envision *Deity* with Frank Harris as a Methodist preacher, for example, or Church of God. You see? Everything changes, not just the three big scenes with Harris himself. Such preachers don't necessarily bring a lot of gravitas to the table; almost the opposite, sometimes. The mother Church has its problems, but its ancient aura does lend a necessary weight and ballast to the unbelievable events here. I don't think there's any doubt about it.

I also decided to go with the Catholic priest *now,* after the extended scene in which Blaine hits the books, getting up to speed on the Judeo-Christian tradition, because what the story really needs at this juncture is not education but confrontation, and with a person, not with a book. Any real novelist would automatically think in these terms, but it took me a while to catch on. (That said, I'm gratified that I haven't heard one complaint about the technical passages throughout *Deity* in which Blaine just sits at his desk studying. In fact, I regret a loss of nerve on my part. I cut quite a few other somewhat esoteric passages, and for a terrible reason: I didn't trust my readers. Only with the novel's success have I realized that those of you who'd pick up such a novel on such a subject in the first place understand that all these issues of divinity aren't so easy. You accept that Blaine would naturally study Church history and biblical exegesis and theology as his self-knowledge and self-appreciation grow, and you seem to enjoy looking over his shoulder. Despite everything, many people in this country and elsewhere still do want to learn.)

Father Frank Harris works at a parish church, and he's completely flummoxed, as we'd expect, by this young man's alleged situation when Blaine broaches it in Harris's rectory as they settle down with their coffee. In that first conversation, however, I didn't think Harris or any other priest would get bogged down in his incorrect assumption of this guy's craziness—time enough for that later—so he allows Blaine to steer the conversation in the direction Blaine (and the story) needs, that is, into a serious consideration of Blaine's own doubts about the miracle in the hospital, the nature of miracles, and what exactly any messiah or deity would have to do in this day and age to prove his bona fides.

Many, many readers have commented on the moment in this scene in which Blaine calmly levitates the lamp on Father Harris's desk. It's a powerful one, I agree, so powerful, in fact, that as I was working on it I gave serious consideration to turning my nascent novel into a play, for the sake of that scene alone, which I still think would be pure dynamite in a theater. On the stage, after all the preliminary theological discourse between the new deity and the humble parish priest, pushing just to the edge of our tolerance for such matters, Blaine would remain quiet for ten, probably fifteen, maybe even twenty seconds, with the audience not really understanding what's going on. And then a few people . . . a few more . . . a critical mass . . . finally the whole theater is murmuring as everyone realizes that the lamp is lifting slowly . . . oh so slowly . . . off the desk. It takes more long moments for the priest to understand what's happening. Blaine watches carefully.

I used to work for two famous movie producers, David Brown and Richard Zanuck, one of whom, David, told me that a few such moments in a movie or a play are all it takes to clinch the deal with the audience. I think he's right. Even now, as I enjoy in my memory *The Godfather, Part 1; Body Heat;* and *Shakespeare in Love,* for example, specific moments come to mind with each: Marlon Brando's expression and hand gesture after Robert Duval tells him how things went down out on the West Coast, concluding with the horse's severed head beneath the purple silk sheets of the mogul's bed; when Mickey Rourke's character reminds his lawyer, Ned Racine (William Hurt), that fifty things can go wrong with even a "decent" crime, and a genius can think of maybe twenty-five—"and you ain't no genius"; and the throw-away line in the rank Elizabethan tavern in which the waiter is describing all the trendy ingredients in today's pig's-foot special. Plays also crystallize in this way—and *Deity* would have been one of them—but the crucial moments in plays are usually more extended, like the first five-iron scene in *True West,* or the black-board scene in *Wit.* But with novels, I usually have to search my memory for any such specific moments, much less attach to them supreme importance for my overall reading pleasure. I've thought a lot about this, and the reason I come up with for the difference is that the printed page is a much more dense environment than either a play or a movie. In a novel, we're burdened with many more moments from which to choose—every sentence is a moment, in this sense, and a really good clause might be one. These moments are not visual, either, not at first. They're handled by different path-ways, so they don't fix in the brain with as much immediacy and potency as an image on the big screen or the big stage.

Or is this analysis just totally wrong? My friend Fred W., also a wordsmith, says yes and cites, off the top, Lady Brett's crossed legs in *The Sun Also Rises* and the curtains of Jay Gatsby's beachside mansion fluttering in the sea breeze. Two good rejoinders, to which I'll even add a third, the scene in John's Gospel in which Jesus tells the scribes and the Pharisees at the Mount of Olives that only he who is without sin should cast the first stone at the adulterous woman. Before that admonition, however, Jesus pauses to write with his finger on the ground, and then he pauses after the admonition and writes in the dirt again. What in the world is going on here?! A lot of people think he's jotting down the sins of these scribes and Pharisees, but I'm not sure. What a delicious mystery, what a singular moment in the prose world, I admit, but I still say that as powerful as the lamp scene in the novel of *The*

Deity Next Door apparently is, in some ways I regret the loss of the overwhelming moment I'm sure it would have been on the stage. As we saw two thousand years ago, the professionals are always the hardest to convince, while many of the folks in the pews are more than willing to believe. This is proved every day, and I'm pretty sure the people in the theater seats—orchestra, balcony, everywhere—would have gasped during this lamp scene. So now we have this undercurrent for the rest of the play—novel—this conflict between the pros and the laity.

I don't think Blaine had prepared for this moment with the lamp. I don't think he'd planned any sort of demonstration. I think he did it on the spur of the moment, but after a pause the length of which I'd leave to the discretion of the actors, but which I think could be quite long, he'd say to Harris, You're thinking magic, aren't you, not miracles? Harris would slowly nod. The two men implicitly understand that one reason miracles don't cut it anymore is that events of the nature just demonstrated will always be challenged as magic, and no psychic or spoon bender has ever been able to accomplish his feats under the controlled circumstances imposed by Harry Houdini or the Incredible Randi, scourges of the supernatural. You can check it out. Nor will these psychics and spoon benders ever be able to, because they're practicing legerdemain. A footnote in Blaine's *Oxford Annotated Bible,* a liberal commentary left over from my own college work, argues that we have to accept the element of the miraculous in the Bible because it was an integral part of the writers' world, because the ancients didn't even have a concept of the uniformity of nature. Today we do share such a concept, and this antisupernatural presupposition (sorry for the mouthful, but that's what it's called) holds sway. We know the naturalistic truth behind each of the ten plagues God visited on Pharaoh: the frogs, gnats, and flies of the second, third, and fourth plagues, for example, were annual proliferations, timed with the seasonal surges of the river Nile. The *Ryrie Study Bible,* a favorite study aid of the evangelicals I know in Texas and the other main source consulted by Blaine, can only acknowledge the natural causes for the plagues while arguing that God multiplied their odious effects to emphasize His supernatural powers.

Go ahead, Blaine tells the priest calmly, gesturing. Harris knows what Blaine is implying and slowly passes his hand underneath the lamp, on top of it, all around. In a play, this scene would need a fine actor to convey the priest's doubt, fear, embarrassment, and maybe a little awe as he gingerly passes his hand slowly around the lamp, checking for wires, fishing line, whatever. With such an actor (Anthony Hopkins or Sean Connery or one of the other weighty Brits is the obvious choice, but what about our own Nathan Lane as a sleeper?) this would be a really powerful moment, followed with perfect timing by a bit of comic relief as

Blaine (Matthew Broderick?) lets the lamp suddenly drop a few inches, threatening to break it, definitely breaking the spell in the theater. He smiles wryly and gazes toward the rapt audience, which would erupt in nervous laughter (or would this irony ruin everything?).

When an embarrassed Father Harris announces abruptly that the alleged miracles of churchmen nominated for sainthood are subjected to the sternest scrutiny that can take many years (a much sterner scrutiny than Christ ever received in the gospel stories, that's for sure), Blaine's reply is my reply: collect the evidence, do the interviews, draw your best conclusion. What takes ten years or even longer? And as far as this particular miracle goes, Blaine adds, you have your own proof right here. (This remark is a little out of character, but it's too late now.) In the early drafts of this scene I also had a long exchange on the question why it's always the Catholics performing the miracles. Why no Protestants? They've had almost five hundred years, but still not one miracle of any renown. And the Jews? Nothing for two thousand years. I'm surprised those pages lasted as long as they did.

The funeral passing in the snowy light outside the window of Father Harris's rectory was a late but necessary addition to the scene because I needed an impulse for the priest to turn to Blaine and ask with some rancor if he could raise someone from the dead. A lamp is just a lamp, and raising it maybe not much more than a cheap parlor trick, but unspoken in this new question is the understanding that the raising of Lazarus from the dead is *the* iconic miracle in the New Testament, the one with the most profound repercussions for Christian theology. The priest's question stops you in your tracks as convincingly as the levitation scene.

The story as told in the Gospel of John is

only forty-four verses long.* In case you've forgotten: Lazarus, the brother of Mary and
Martha, has been lying in his tomb for four
days by the time Jesus arrives in Bethany to
pay his respects. Mary and Martha accost him,
charging that if he'd come earlier Lazarus
wouldn't have died; Jesus would have healed
him. Their distress is understandable, but popular belief in the ancient world imagined the
soul's lingering near the body for three days
before departing for wherever, so the *four* days
in the tomb for Lazarus were necessary to
accentuate the miraculousness of the event.
When Jesus declares that Martha's brother
will rise again, she understandably misinter-
prets the statement and replies that yes, he'll
rise again in the resurrection on the last day (a
common belief among devout Jews in those
days). This is when Jesus responds with his
famous claim that he is the resurrection and

---

*John 11:1–44.

the life, and that whoever believes in him shall live even if he dies. The poor woman still doesn't comprehend Jesus's claim, so when he orders that the stone blocking the entrance of Lazarus's tomb be removed, she gently reminds him that there will be a stench. Jesus ignores her and cries for Lazarus to step forth, which he does, still in his funeral wrappings. Jesus says simply, Unbind him, and let him go.

In Dallas, I heard the famous, late Southern Baptist preacher W. A. Criswell deliver a spellbinding sermon on Lazarus. After his brisk narration of the story he paused in ominous silence for long seconds before demanding to know whether the modern existentialist could raise Lazarus from the dead. What about the sophomoric spiritual sophist? Or the professional paid religionist (the great line quoted earlier as a typically conservative Protestant view of Catholicism; Criswell's funny if nasty description of gorgeous vestments, incense, and foreign incantations left no doubt regarding the object of his scorn)? What about the philosophical rationalist and the pseudoscientist, with their empty, stupid, unthinkable hypothesis of evolution? Furthermore, our preacher demanded, could any of these ladies and gentlemen tell us *who* we are, *where* we came from, *where* we're going, and *why*?! It's laughable to think so. Then why in the world reject *He who can* tell us these things?! He who *already has*?!

Criswell glared at his congregation. We were chagrined. I've never forgotten that fine moment in the pulpit, and I was thinking of it while Blaine was wondering if indeed *he* could have raised his son Tim from the dead, had he not cured him instead. He replies to Father Harris that maybe he would have to raise someone, or at least try, and, sure, he'd be nervous. When Harris asks if Blaine intends to accomplish this by sneaking into a morgue, and when he asks what happens if he's successful, because things could get a little sticky, explanations would be required—with these questions, the good father can't hide the sarcasm. On the stage he would stop, shake his head, smile ruefully. What the hell is going on here? Is he actually taking this guy seriously? Yes, he is, and now I have a ready-made, ongoing teaser for the rest of *Deity*. How often does a cemetery enter the story in some way? At least half a dozen times, from the brief moment when Blaine pauses beside the cemetery behind Trinity Church to the graveside service for Father Harris late in the story. There are cemeteries all over the place, and the one morgue, of course, and with every reference I hope you thought about Lazarus—and about Blaine. Is he finally going to do it?

You've asked me if Blaine himself is headed for the grave, or does his divinity entail immortality? The truth is I hadn't thought about the question until the first time I encountered it in Seattle. Yes, I replied quickly, divinity probably entails immortality, but then the guy pointed out that Blaine apparently looks his age—mid-thirties—so he's aging physically, isn't he? If his story should fail to end apocalyptically, what happens as the centuries roll by? This fellow had really worked up his argument, and he got the best of me. I don't know the answer, frankly, and the conclusion of *Deity* dodges the problem without realizing it's doing so.

Finally, regarding this pivotal first scene with Father Harris, did you notice that it's the first time I establish an explicit season for the story, with Harris standing up after the business with the lamp and watching the funeral procession roll away just as the snowflakes have begun to fall? This seemed like the right opportunity and the right season. Ninety degrees and high humidity weren't appropriate, for the same reason they weren't appropriate for the gestation of Judaism and Christianity—and then of Islam. All three faiths are simply inconceivable as expressions of a *tropical* culture. No way. Or, to come at it from the perspective not of secular anthropology but of religious belief, why did God choose these desert tribes as opposed to a tropical people for special status? We can surmise that He knew, thanks to omniscience, that these particular cultures of Palestine and the Levant were the ones that were going somewhere—or at least could go somewhere, given half a chance—for the reasons developed at length by Jared Diamond in *Guns, Germs, and Steel* (another unexpected megaseller), whereas the residents of Borneo, to take just one example, would be restricted almost to the starting line by their isolated, humid, equatorial environs. What would have been the point of choosing them?! This sounds irreverent, but within the context of the Judeo-Christian claim, it's a perfectly fair question, and, I think, a provocative one.

So why is Blaine based in the *New* World? This somewhat less provocative question has been raised a few times, and the answer begins with the old adage they're always telling new novelists, to write what you know. This strategy cuts both ways, depending on what you know, so with *Deity* I decided to play it safe. Since I was writing about something—divinity—about which I don't know anything except through hearsay, I'd at least set the story someplace I do know about, New York City, capital of the New World. The other, better reason Blaine lives in New York is that America is where it's happening today. We're setting the course, for better or worse. The esteemed old cultures of Palestine and the Levant have passed the torch. What would have been the point of choosing one of them, or even somewhere in Europe?

Harris doesn't know what to make of Blaine. The damned lamp was floating, no doubt about that—there weren't any wires. But who is this Blaine what's-his-name, and what's going on in the rest of his life? All fair questions, Father Harris decides. Meanwhile, Blaine walks home in his own state of confusion. The meeting with the priest hasn't answered any questions at all—has only raised more of them. It has achieved one object, however: he was able to levitate the lamp under the pressure of observation, something he'd never tried before. True, he hadn't told Harris ahead of time that he'd levitate the lamp, so if he hadn't succeeded Harris wouldn't have known this. Still, he'd done it and definitely given the priest something to think about. But the whole thing seems so ridiculous, Blaine reminds himself. How the hell could I really be some kind of deity or messiah? Or do I just have the paranormal powers that the spoon benders have only pretended to have? Nowhere is it written that levitating lamps requires divinity. But the healing—that's beyond the merely paranormal, isn't it?—but not if you're a Christian Scientist—if it really *was* healing, because terminally ill patients do occasionally pull through.

Blaine is utterly lost. An ambulance wails

past, and he watches it weave in and out of traffic before it disappears down Ninth Avenue. Why didn't I heal that woman? Blaine knows she had fallen down the stairs of her town house on West Twenty-first Street and struck her head on the banister. (This scene of mundane omniscience was inspired by an old mystery story I'd worked on many years before, in which the private detective is driving down the freeway watching a black Lab riding on the rear bumper of a Chevy pickup—not in the bed of the pickup, where dogs are always riding, but outside on the bumper. The closed tailgate serves as a backstop for any forward lurches, but there's nothing at the rear between the dog and oblivion. He's glancing around with his brilliant black eyes, long ears flapping furiously, inches from death, barking with joy. (One morning in Houston, where I lived at the time, I actually saw this dog, the model for Blaine's beloved chocolate Lab, Gore-Tex.) Everyone in the cars surrounding the Chevy pickup is awestruck, among them a young woman in a Jaguar with a double Ph.D. in linguistics and cultural anthropology from Wisconsin-Milwaukee who's on her way to a tryst in which she betrays her husband, an older man who worships the ground she walks on and would have bought her not just this Jaguar but the entire dealership, if that had been her desire. "In my line of work at the time," the private detective narrates, "you tend to understand people at a glance." Of course, he has no idea who this woman is, or where she's going in her Jaguar, or for what purpose. He's just amusing himself and (I hoped) the reader. But, I now wondered many years later, what if the new deity isn't just amusing himself when he generates such sudden insight?)

I always ask audiences how many miracles are described in the gospels, and the hesitant answers—"Four or five?" "Ten?" "Maybe a dozen?"—are always too low. The *Ryrie Study Bible* calculates the number at thirty-five, and many of those are general references to multiple episodes, so there were a lot of miracles—but still not enough, because most of the people of Palestine never accepted Jesus as the messiah. So why didn't he therefore perform more miracles? Pacing the streets, Blaine wants to know. Why not as many miracles as necessary to convince every hardheaded Jew in Judea and Samaria, and maybe all the pagans as well? Lord *knows* Jesus could have convinced the whole world, but he didn't. Why not? It's a prominent question. Could Blaine have helped this woman in the ambulance? Could or should he have saved every kid in the hospital, every kid in the world? Prominent questions, and his mind boils with confusion and doubt, and that's the reason the prose in this section is a little overheated itself.

Talk about temptations, he's flooded with them: surely a real deity would be made of sterner stuff than this one exhibits when he peremptorily changes a traffic light in his favor. Or maybe these tribulations just reflect how much the world has changed in two thousand years, how an age of unbelief would affect the mind and psyche of even a deity. It's clear in the Bible that Jesus was a man of his time as well as the Son of God. Today, wouldn't Blaine be a man of *his* time as well as the Son of God? But wait a minute, Blaine exclaims. What does any of this have to do with anything? Could I save the world—or put an end to it—right now? Isn't this the one question that it all comes down to? If I can, then I'm the real thing; if I can't, then I'm something else. *What would Jesus do?!* I should know that answer by now—but I don't— I'm as bad as Hamlet. (The embedded citation is from the scene with the players, act II, scene ii.)

During his brief career on Earth, Jesus was totally committed regarding his identity and his powers, but who knows what he went through during the first dozen years of his adult life? There could be a lot of parallels between those unknown years and Blaine's dilemma in *Deity,* we just don't know. Maybe Jesus doubted, maybe he didn't, but Blaine simply has to. Who wouldn't today?! I was convinced this was the correct analysis, but my friend Paul P., a lifelong student of comparative religion who knows a lot more about all this than I do, warned me to be careful. In the first place, Paul pointed out, deity requires self-knowledge, by definition. Second, a deity of slowly dawning consciousness might bring to mind for some well-read readers the Eastern idea of the man waking up to the Buddha within himself. The famous phrase, "If you meet the Buddha on the road, kill him," emphasizes that the external Buddha is of no avail if you don't have an internal Buddha with whom to greet him. Was any such implied discourse between Eastern and Western conceptions of the sacred what I wanted in *The Deity Next Door*? Not until you brought it up, Paul!

I took the advice to be careful, but I couldn't alter my basic conviction: for Jesus Christ, divinity would make instant, eminent sense, but what in the world is Blaine doing here as a deity today, when nobody really cares—but "cares" may not be quite right—when no one is paying any attention. Such are Blaine's thoughts as he goes about his business, and that's why he's of a mind to test himself further. I can levitate a lamp? I even had something to do with curing my son of cancer? I have that power of prayer or whatever? If I'm crazy enough to believe this, I'm crazy enough to try it again. These boiling doubts are the motivation behind the miraculous cure of the second boy on the same floor at Sloan-Kettering that Tim had been on, but this time from a different kind of cancer.

We can't be certain why we're reading

about this second boy with cancer, but when the remission occurs we should somehow intuit that Blaine is involved, even though he's back home with Melanie and Tim. This is a more spine-tingling moment than the first cure, or so I hope, and it's also spine-tingling for Blaine. He goes ahead and calls the hospital to confirm the news, but he knows that the other little boy has been unexpectedly sent home. He just knows. Something big *is* going on, and as a private celebration, almost, he goes out on the streets and asks the guys if he can shoot a few baskets and immediately scores from twenty-five, and then again, and again, and then from half-court, as the silence deepens on the court. I'd thrown out the early baseball scene, but I was determined to get some sports into the earlier pages. That's the main reason Blaine shoots those hoops, and it's also why I maneuver him into the round of golf with the psychiatrist a few pages later. I enjoy this game, and writing about Blaine's pleased realization that he can smash his drive five hundred yards was visceral fun. I could feel his pleasure within my own body as I typed, because there's something about a prodigious drive (probably the fact that I can't hit one).

Now, recall the sentence in which Blaine apprehends that he could power the ball not just five hundred yards but five thousand yards, or five thousand *miles,* or "the width of the universe, for that matter." To my mind, that phrase is one of the more important in the novel. For the first thirty-three pages I've kept the focus pretty tight, trying to keep the reader wrapped in the here and now of Blaine's developing story, suppressing for the time being its awesome implications—but suddenly this reference to the cosmic scale, which should open those implications with a powerful rush, while also implicitly undercutting them because we're talking about a Titleist golf ball.

Fundamentalists like to accost the casually unobservant with the assertion that Jesus Christ was either mad, bad, or God, one of the three, take your choice, and they hope your cultural conscience will inhibit you from saying that Jesus was either mad or bad. If so, you're cornered, but if so it's your own fault, because there's a fourth plausible choice: Jesus Christ was a charismatic man transformed by cultural forces we can't imagine into the legendary and literary creation we meet in the Gospels. And even if he *was* God, problems remain. One cause of Blaine's confusion regarding his own deity in the first third or so of *The Deity Next Door* is the damnably difficult question that has bedeviled thoughtful Christians from the beginning: the real nature of Jesus Christ. The answer to this question about Jesus should, or at least might, hold for Blaine as well, and while it seems to boil down to one question—was Jesus divine?—it's not nearly as simple as that if you take your Christianity straight and not, as C. S. Lewis so famously quipped, with water.

The specifics about Christian divinity are complicated because they're so closely bound up with the requirements for redemption and salvation—which is, after all, the official purpose of the faith. Jesus must be divine in order to fulfill his salvific mission, because a mere man couldn't redeem us, but he must also embody sinful humanity in order that he understand and feel our need for salvation in the first place. Therefore, Jesus can't be just man or just God, but both at the same time, a profound puzzle for the earliest Christian thinkers. It's no surprise that heresies were rife: Jesus was only a man, or only God, or some kind of demigod, or some other entity. Scripture wasn't helpful, either, because every opinion could find corroboration somewhere in the Gospels or the letters of Paul. For starters, the appellation "Son of Man," used by Jesus himself over eighty times, had the meaning in Jewish culture of "mortal man" or, at the most, a messianic figure;[*] no one argues that it necessarily connoted divinity. Nor did the term "messiah" (or the Greek translation, "Christ"), who would be a figure of apocalyptic importance—a deliverer, a redeemer, a chosen man, a king of kings, a worker of miracles, even— but not necessarily divine.

On the other hand, supreme divinity *is* posited by John in the justly famous first verse of his gospel, which identifies Christ with the divine wisdom of the Logos, so it was all complicated for the early Christians trying to codify the essentials of the new faith. And they played for keeps. Troops were called out on

---

[*]Daniel 7:13: "I kept looking in the night visions, and behold, with the clouds of heaven one like a Son of Man was coming, and He came up to the Ancient of Days and was presented before Him."

more than one occasion to quell disturbances; anathemas and condemnations were issued with alacrity. Courts of inquiry exiled, reinstated, and reexiled various clergymen, depending on the fluctuating fortunes of their particular dogmas. Athanasius, bishop of Alexandria and chief supporter of the orthodoxy still embodied in the Athanasian Creed, was officially exiled at least three times, forced into hiding on other occasions, and falsely prosecuted for a host of crimes, including murder (a rap he beat when the alleged victim was discovered in hiding). If I were looking for a subject for a second bestseller (or for a first hit play), Athanasius's career might be my choice. It's eventful in the extreme, as well as ideal for dramatizing the doctrinal chaos that distinguished the early centuries—not years, as most people innocently believe, but centuries—of the new religion.

In the end, the big conference in Chalcedon in 451 hammered out the official Christological doctrine: Jesus Christ was complete both in his deity *and* in his humanity, both truly God *and* truly man, all at the same time. Accept it. But does this have-it-both-ways stance really hold up to inspection? Can our minds—ancient or modern—understand the purest immanence and the purest transcendence incorporated in one being? Can we understand such mixing of oil and water? I certainly can't, and I haven't met or read anyone who I think really does. (Nevertheless, I nominate this doctrine of Hypostatic Union as one of the two most important political compromises in our history, along with the U.S. Constitution.)

It's easy enough to disdain the Christological debate—I think again of Hamlet ("Words, words, words"), and I have sympathy for Tertullian's suggestion that the absurdity is integral to the truth of the Christian faith—but the issue was serious business in those early days of the Church (proof enough of the vast difference in faith as experienced then and now), it's serious today within a tiny academic circle, and it was serious for me while I was trying to create the character of Blaine in *Deity*. Not *if* Blaine is divine, but *how*? I gave this more time than any other problem, and the more confused I became the higher my admiration for the Gospel writers, who skate us right over the parallel problems with Jesus Christ, which just don't seem to matter while we're reading their stories. It's only when we put the Gospels down that the questions step forth for consideration.

I'm no expert, but I'm prepared to accept the hypothesis that it was Shakespeare who virtually invented the idea of character in literature that we now take for granted in our plays, novels, movies, and even some TV shows. Such characterization wasn't the aspiration or the achievement of any of the great literatures of the ancient world. In the Gospels, we don't really know Jesus as a fully rounded man. We're presented with different character traits—anger, sadness, and deepest compassion, mainly—but only as they relate to his carefully delimited role. There's no attempt by any of the four writers to portray Jesus's full humanity, or to give a complete picture of his emotional life. There's no attempt to *get inside him.* The idea never occurred to those writers, I'm sure. However, I couldn't get away with a stick figure—and by using that loaded term I mean no derogation at all. The Gospels are great, especially Mark, but they had a different purpose for a different audience in a different world from ours. I was obligated to portray a genuine character, or as close to one as I could.

How does Blaine *feel?* What's his interior life really like? When he has one of those moments of sudden, profound psychological insight, or when he levitates the lamp, or when he cures Timothy, does he turn the divinity *on* or does he turn the humanity *off*? Did Jesus do it the same way, or differently? For days I paced the halls and walked the streets, imagining myself as divine—trying to imagine myself as divine—trying to understand how this might feel, how it might actually work in real life. But I got no further than I get when I try to grasp a spatial distance of fifteen billion light-years, or the billion cycles per second of the basic microchip, or the God who understands in every particular the six billion souls alive today, the many more who've gone before, the even more presumably still to come.

Some scholars argue that since the Gospel writers were amateurs, only divine inspiration could account for their utterly convincing narratives in the face of all the difficulties, and I give this point some credence in one respect at least: I do have difficulty picturing those writers making up some of the miracles. The healings, maybe, because miraculous healings were a given in the ancient world. The raising of

Lazarus, or the stilling of the storm,* or the feeding of the five thousand†—these are also plausible to me as the literary artifacts of an oral tradition. But John's story about turning the water into wine at the wedding in Cana?‡ Or the quick story in which Jesus curses the fig tree?§ Where did such strange miracles come from? Now that I've written my own story that required miracles, I find it hard to believe that Matthew said to himself one day at his writing stand, Hey, I think I'll have Jesus wither the leaves on a fig tree, that's a good one. I don't get the sense that he and the others worked like that, maybe because I was tempted to work like that, once or twice. For me, the secret of the Gospels is hidden somewhere in this contradiction: the books—parts of them—may *be*

---

*Matthew 8:23–27; Mark 4:35–41; Luke 8:22–25.

†Matthew 14:14–21; Mark 6:34–44; Luke 9:12–17; John 6:5–13.

‡John 2:1–11.

§Matthew 21:18–19; Mark 11:12–14.

fiction, but Matthew, Mark, Luke, and John were not *writing* fiction.

Whatever the explanation for the Gospels—genius, faith, divine inspiration—I wasn't benefiting from it. I couldn't get a firm grip on Blaine's split personality and eventually gave up trying. One more time, I adopted the strategy of the gospelists: I decided to ignore the problem. I'd never be able to understand Blaine's Man-Godness, and I had no choice but to trust that my readers, modern though you are, would accept my premise on this question, just as you accept Blaine's divinity in the first place. However, I'd reverse the strategies of the Gospels. I'd go easy on the proclamations and evidences of Blaine's deity, develop his humanity instead, and hope that I, too, could distract you from the deep mystery, perhaps even contradiction, at the heart of any earthbound deity, then or now.

Jesus prayed. Why doesn't Blaine pray? Folks think they've tricked me when they spring this one. Surely Blaine would pray if I'm emphasizing his humanity over his divinity—a good point to which I respond with two good ones of my own. First, Blaine doesn't pray after discovering his divinity because he didn't pray beforehand. Second, I've always had problems with the biblical scenes in which Jesus prays. I know that, according to the Talmud, God Himself puts on the phylacteries and prays, and my evangelical friend Jim P. patiently explained that prayer among the three personalities of the Christian Trinity makes perfect sense as a way to communicate, one with the other. (But wait a minute, Jim, what about omniscience? This sounds like a solid rebuttal, but without even asking I know he has an answer, because these well-educated evangelicals always do. You can't trick them. I've tried and seen it tried by others many times, never successfully.) To me, Jesus's prayers testify in favor of the argument that he viewed himself as a man chosen of God, but that's all. I feared that any praying scenes in *Deity* would break the spell of my story, just as they break the spell for me in the Gospels, and would lead my readers to the same conclusion regarding Blaine, that he is chosen of God but not divine per se. I had posited divinity for Blaine, and I didn't want to jeopardize it. I couldn't risk any prayers. I didn't even try one or two, just to see how they'd read. I knew how they'd read.

In the Incarnation, God becomes human and—I don't think this has received enough attention—the human becomes God. This particular way of looking at Blaine's nature opened new possibilities for me—and for Blaine, as he paced the streets and avenues of the city following the first interview with Father Harris, contemplating his own feelings about what he is . . . is not . . . might be . . . should be . . . will be. Thinking back, you'll realize that Blaine now becomes a more active character, no longer hamstrung in the search for some ordained role of old, but seeking a new one that makes more sense to him and us today. To my mind, Blaine's shaving scene is the key one here— and what a fluke it was. I almost always shave in the shower, but one morning, for no reason I can pin down in retrospect, I stood at the sink, and while listening to a piece on *Morning Edition* about the Holy Land I was struck by the metaphorical possibilities of this mundane exercise. I'm glad most readers do interpret that scene in *Deity* as the perfect metaphor for Blaine's dilemma in our modern world, steeped as it is in self-consciousness and doubt: while shaving, he has to look in the mirror every morning, while Jesus didn't have that problem.

For some time I debated whether I should retain the ending I had concocted for this chapter and finally decided, why not? It's kind of a cheap trick, but I was just trying to write an entertaining little tale that might also give us something to think about. Besides, it stands to reason that no Catholic priest is going to take claims of deity lying down. In fact, no priest is going to accept a new deity, period, unless and until he's led kicking and screaming to the proof. Jesus warned his disciples to be careful about being misled, because many would follow him, claiming to be Christ. Today, proof is a much more difficult proposition than it was in the old days. So why not: as Blaine reaches his apartment building at long last, Father Harris picks up the telephone to call his brother, a private detective in Brooklyn.

Chapter Three

JUST AS I SAT at my desk in the apartment on West Twenty-fourth Street writing *The Deity Next Door,* Blaine sat at his desk in the apartment on West Twenty-fourth Street working on the programming problems on which he consulted for a living. (This was pretty much a default career. I didn't really care what Blaine did. Jesus's trade as a carpenter wasn't important, that I can see, nor was I implying the banal point that programming today is the fundamental trade that carpentry was two thousand years ago.) Both of us looked into the rear-facing windows of the apartments in the other, parallel wing of London Terrace that runs along Twenty-third Street. The distance across is just twenty-seven yards. (Both of us measured it in the garden between the wings.) Specifically, we looked into a dozen or so apartments across the way—from two floors below us to two floors above us, and from the "F" line on the left to the "H" line on the right. The full range of New Yorkers live in London Terrace. A lot of people work at home—graphic artists, journalists, almost anything that can be accomplished on the computer—others are in the theatrical trades, and there are a lot of photographers and their models (women about whom you think, With that body, in this culture, do they really have a choice?), and quite a few retired folks. You know these people after a while, though their lives remain full of mystery. Or, I should say, Blaine and I knew some of them, and to us their lives were full of mystery, because neither his wife nor mine paid much attention, and they didn't know that we did.

They thought we were in there working eight hours a day—in Blaine's case, resolving software problems with miraculous dexterity; in mine, resolving editorial problems in my novel about Blaine (without miraculous dexterity).

As much as we enjoyed our real work, both of us had certain instincts that were gratified by the lives on display across the way. We became mesmerized, especially with the gestures, which are so expressive yet ambiguous when seen only as mime. If you can't hear the conversation, you really have no idea what the people mean. The arm slightly uplifted from the side, hand turned slightly upward—it can express acceptance or bewilderment, maybe slight anger. Sometimes I felt I knew which one from observing the other features of the scene—arrangement of bodies, preceding and subsequent movements and expressions—but often it just wasn't possible. One woman was particularly expansive, even animated. For Blaine and me, her arms and hands were her primary means of expression, her words secondary, except during those late-summer nights with the windows open when she paced about the rooms yelling at someone over the telephone in extremely primary language.

She often wore a sleeveless white T-shirt while opening the purple curtains and then the windows in the morning and then closing them in the evening, her long white arms hinged and straining with effort against the tight fit of the sash, her breasts gently squeezed by the soft cotton. How eloquent of homely endeavor! We tried never to miss this particular action, and rarely did, because the curtains did have to be opened and closed every day, along with the windows, even in winter, when we had too much heat in the building, if anything. And what could be lovelier than two women necking? As a man, kissing a woman is great enough, but imagine doing so as another woman! My plump, soft breasts melting into your plump, soft breasts? Imagine how erotic and profound that must be: the mother lode of woman's love. So it's for good reason that the men's magazines often feature lesbians—even we obtuse and benighted males can appreciate the relative purity of this passion—and small wonder the ratings were sky high for the episode of *Ally McBeal* a couple of years ago in which the two stars wonder whether it's better without the man. Frankly, I don't see why more women don't wonder. Or maybe they do—I'll bet they do—yes, they must. In the end, the two co-stars decided that they would miss the male member, if not the rest of him, and that this makes all the difference. I say . . . maybe.

As it happened on West Twenty-third Street, I saw only the one scene that got out of hand between the woman in the white T-shirt and her lover—the inspiration, obviously, for the most notorious of the temptation scenes in *Deity.* You can bet that my editor and I had a long conversation about the advisability of including this particular action—it's such a guy thing, and women, who buy most of the novels in this country, and almost all of the good ones, are offended, but I kept the scene anyway, to emphasize Blaine's red-blooded straight American maleness. Also, some kind of temptation scenes were a given, because we all know about them in the Bible. There's nothing about the sexual temptation of Jesus in the Gospels, but there's plenty about sexual temptation in other contexts—the apostle Paul, for one, is famously obsessed by the subject, with liberal commentators blaming mainly him and then Augustine for the Church's deep suspicion of women and its relegation of them to subservient status within its precincts. (In all fairness, I'd argue that Christianity has done better by its women than, for example, Islam, although you could reply that the huge picture of Kate Moss splayed across the top of Times Square is as demeaning as any burka.) Kazantzakis modernized the temptations in his blockbuster, especially with the scene in Mary Magdalene's brothel, so I don't think my decision to include a little sexual temptation was in any way a craven capitulation to the prevailing taste of modern readers.

In the Gospels, the temptations were necessary to demonstrate that Jesus was genuinely tempted (in his role as a human, he has to be), but he doesn't sin, not even in his heart, because as the Son of God he can't. So he's fully human except for this one key difference. For his part, Blaine has no reason to prove his sinlessness, which wouldn't serve any salvific or other theological purpose. No, his chief temptation has been not believing in himself—this has been pretty much the driving force behind the story to this point—while a secondary issue has been his ego. This scene with the two women and the other implicit temptation scenes scattered here and there in *Deity*—on the basketball court, Blaine's temptation to score from the other end of the court; on the golf course, to put his long-hitting opponent to shame; in the hospital, to cure everyone; with Melanie, to preen as the indefatigable lover; with his high-tech clients, to solve their asymmetric, multithreaded problems literally overnight; every time he passes a cemetery, to raise the dead; toward the end of the story, to give in to the siren call of celebrity—all such temptations I thought of as Blaine's efforts to control his blossoming ego, mirroring what some commentators see as an evolution in God's handling of His own ego in the centuries between those outbursts of unflattering pique in the Old Testament and the coming of Jesus Christ.

In Matthew and Luke, Jesus, after his forty days in the wilderness, is tempted by the devil to prove his divinity by turning stones into bread, and then by leaping off a pinnacle so that angels may save him. Jesus refuses to participate in any such demonstration of his glory. From the vantage of a high mountain,

Satan then offers Jesus all the kingdoms of the world, if only he'll worship Satan. Jesus refuses. (I've mentioned my late friend Roy N., the writer who specialized in horseplay and who wrote that ill-fated "Sports Journal" piece. In *Buffalopia,* one of Roy's funniest unproduced screenplays, Indians discover Europe in 1492, passing Columbus on the Atlantic Ocean heading this way, but before the Indians set sail one of the chiefs takes his son to a high vantage in the Adirondacks, spreads his arms wide and declares with all solemnity, "Someday, son, none of this will be yours." Great line, poignant in that context and in this one: two thousand years ago, who could have guessed the incredible ascendance of the Christian faith for eighteen or so centuries, and now this sudden decline in most of the Western world to its status as cultural artifact?)

Given that Satan is behind the temptations of Jesus, why doesn't Satan figure into Blaine's temptations as well? Common question, and the simple answer is that I decided that accepting Satan's explicit presence would be too much of a stretch for too many readers. In a comedy, fine, but not in *The Deity Next Door*. Of course, many readers who wouldn't accept Satan and his cohort of demons would welcome angels, but there aren't any of them in *Deity*, either, out of fairness. I had no intention of catering to those Christians who demean their religion (in my humble opinion) by treating it as a cafeteria, choosing which doctrines they'll believe, which they won't, which are important, which aren't, and which are too troublesome to even think about. (Mormons refer to this last category as "shelf doctrines," and they should know.)

As it happened, the apartment with the action between the two women became empty shortly after it had served its purpose for me. I'd seen certain signs of a move-out for a couple of weeks but somehow hadn't paid much attention until one day some guys showed up with boxes. Within hours everyone was gone and the apartment was vacant. The following morning the painters were already there, but then the apartment remained empty for a while—a number of weeks, unusual in Manhattan at that time. When the new tenants finally moved in, well, they were disappointing. A young couple taking care of their young boy versus the two women? That was no contest, but I couldn't help noting a few salient facts about the newcomers nevertheless, living as they were directly across from my desk. The guy worked at home on his computer, but I saw only the back of the machine, so I really couldn't get an idea if he was yet another graphic designer, or a writer, or a software programmer, or what. His wife was also there most of the time, taking care of their son, who was just about old enough for kindergarten.

A couple of weeks passed, during which I was making very little progress with *Deity*. Then one morning, out of the blue, when I wasn't particularly focused on either my neighbors or my novel, I glanced across the way and was startled by the realization that the young man with the wife and son looked exactly like Blaine. To that point in my writing, I hadn't described the next messiah closely, hadn't even thought about the question much because such descriptions in other novels have never done me much good. I think readers want to know if a man has a beard or a mustache, or if a woman has long blond hair or a crew cut, but a description without such distinguishing and telltale characteristics is just words. This is especially true in an era of visual images, when the words can't compete, so why even try? Blaine had no remarkable characteristics, I hadn't described him (and never would), but I must have had a picture in my mind's eye nevertheless, because there he suddenly was right in front of me—or at least my realization was in that instant.

You can imagine my surprise. My heart skipped a beat, and then another. By now, you know I'm pretty down-to-earth and not prone to go overboard on this kind of thing, but I was truly spooked by my discovery. How could this be, what could this mean? Just as the real world had projected itself into my story in any number of ways, some of them told here, I now wondered whether my story was somehow projecting itself out into the real world—a grandiose sentiment, but I can't deny that it crossed my mind. My man Blaine, his wife Melanie, their young son Tim—and now this look-alike across the way, his pretty wife, his beloved son: the most radical of my inflamed hypotheses was that this new tenant was the next messiah *in fact*, not in fiction, that he had divinely recruited me to serve unwittingly as his John the Baptist by writing the "novel" that would indirectly break the ice and introduce him—the idea of him—to the public. A week or so later, when my laptop crashed, somehow taking with it both the backup floppy and the Zip drive, costing me three days' hard work, I wondered if I was being tested.

Finally, though, I was able to settle down and get back to work—except that now I could hardly take my eyes off those six windows across the way. Weeks went by, and the new family turned out to be an unexceptional one. Mom and dad closed the curtains when they should have, kept things neat and tidy, worked hard. No levitating lamps, either, that I could see. The guy may have looked like Blaine, but he wasn't Blaine. Occasionally I saw him or the whole family on the street and came away with the same impression: nice people, regular folks, diligent parents, cute kid.

And then another surprise: just three or four months after the family moved in, they closed up the apartment. They didn't move, but just loaded some boxes, put stuff away, covered the sofa, and were gone the next day. The place was dark. I immediately made inquiries of the concierge staff and learned that the Riley family (not their real name) had temporarily left for Houston—Houston? that's my home town—to be nearer "some big cancer hospital they have down there, some real special cancer." M.D. Anderson Hospital. For a second time regarding this couple, my heart and my mind raced, and back at my desk, within an hour, I'm not kidding, the phrase "the deity next door" came to mind as a potential title. It was hokey, but I liked it immediately, and the timing suggests that in some manner I still related the guy across the way to Blaine.

A little over a month later I was in Houston, where my parents still live in the house I grew up in. Visiting them was my purpose, but I knew I'd go by M.D. Anderson to see if I could find out anything about the Riley couple, who would have brought their young son to the hospital some weeks before. That information is confidential, the nurse I finally ended up with said. Look, I pleaded, I'm a writer working on a story (*ugh,* but I didn't think I had any choice) and, well, it's complicated, but this kid is involved in my story, in a way. I really need to find this family. Is there any way at all? Not really, she replied, but maybe a lawyer could help. Are you a Christian? I asked. You are?! My story is about a Second Coming of sorts and this young boy's father looks exactly like the messiah character in my story, and long before I saw this family I had a scene in which the messiah cures his son of cancer, and then he cures another boy on the same floor. Doesn't it seem like a remarkable coincidence to you that this man now brings his son all the way from New York to M.D. Anderson in Houston, which happens to be my home town? Aren't you interested in finding out whether this boy's cancer has gone into remission, perhaps inexplicably, maybe along with another boy's on the same floor?

I'll never forget the look on that woman's face, but I knew from experience that Christians—serious Christians—often have a wonderful sweetness about them even as they're consigning you to hell, and I thought this sweetness and a dollop of curiosity might win out over my obvious lunacy in this lady's mind. We looked at each other in silence for quite a while, or so it seemed, though how long could it have been, five seconds? ten? Finally she said, surely in violation of all rules and regulations, Call me tomorrow. When I did so, I got the surprise that trumped all the others. Indeed, a couple named Riley and their son from New York City had come to M.D. Anderson, but it was the father who had cancer—the *father,* not the son, as I'd assumed because that scenario lined up with my story. The clerk paused, and I knew she had more news for me—bad news. Indeed. The patient had died in a nearby hospice.

The air was sucked from my lungs, the floor began to tilt and wobble, a void opened before me. Nor could I say a word. The *messiah* had died? That's what it felt like to me.

When I then called my brother Ralph, a private detective in Houston, to find out if he had any time to follow up on the matter of John Riley, he'd just been hired by a woman who had come into his office and announced that her husband was seeing another woman almost every Tuesday afternoon, sometimes on Thursday. (There might have been other times as well, but it didn't matter.) Her husband met this woman in the parking lot of the Galleria, the famous shopping mall in Houston. He waited in his limousine; she arrived in her Jaguar, parked, and got into his limo. They drove somewhere, returned several hours later, and she got back in her car and both left. The guy's wife now wanted documentation of this illicit rendezvous.

Coincidentally, Ralph had just read a magazine article about private investigators that mentioned that you can sit at the perimeter of the parking lot at any large shopping center in this country and within an hour almost certainly see someone arrive in one car, alone, and depart in another one, and then, if you want to wait a while, you'll see the return of the second car and the final departure of both cars. Happens hourly, according to the article, and here it was in Ralph's new career. My brother had been a photographer for years, and that turned out to be what his newest client wanted: photographs. She also wanted some kind of proof of the date in the frame, so Ralph planned to position the front page of the *Chronicle* in the foreground of his shots. At least this would establish an earliest possible date for the tryst. I ended up going along for the ride that afternoon, the job came off perfectly, and I knew then and there that I needed detectives in *The Deity Next Door*, which could be called a theological thriller, in essence, just as *Hamlet* could be called a political thriller. (I didn't want to go that far—in my favorite play, just about everyone spies on everyone else, directly or indirectly—but how could a detective or two not help my story?) My brother became the model for the character of Father Harris's brother Ralph, the private detective from Brooklyn who checks out Blaine, but not the model for the detective hired by Melanie, when she later becomes so concerned about Blaine's bizarre behavior. That evening I also wrote the scene in which Blaine roams the tarmac outside the shopping center, interviewing all the shoppers, losing his cool, and ending up in jail for the night.

But tell me if I've oversold the story of

John Riley and his untimely death from cancer. Were you hoping for something supernatural? I must have been at the time, and I'm betting that you were, too, as you read the story just now. History shows that it's not difficult for us to slip into this hopeful frame of mind—a propensity that must be at least partly responsible for the success of *The Deity Next Door*. But alas, nothing of the kind happened in the case of John Riley. He wasn't the real next messiah, as far as I know. Like Blaine, he'd been a software consultant, and the quiet life I'd witnessed for the four months he and his family had lived across from us in New York was his only life. No astonishing secrets, according to Ralph, and when I drove out to Forest Glen to visit the grave of this man whom I'd never met, nothing special happened. Nevertheless, the novel I was writing would never be the same.

The reason the folks at the Bible college in Dallas thought I was a closeted Christian was that they thought I understood them better than most outsiders they encountered. In this they were correct. I did understand them and their faith, but I was still restrained by the absence of the deepest emotional connection. I didn't understand this until years after I wrote that book—until this episode with the deity next door, John Riley, who wasn't the deity next door. I must have wanted that man to be the messiah, maybe even needed it, for the sake of my work in progress, if nothing else; now I really understood the Christian faith. Quite simply, it wagers everything on the power of a single *person*—Jesus Christ—to define and change lives.

Wasn't it Diana Vreeland, the late editor of *Vogue,* who said that, at bottom, people are only interested in other people? That's not true of everyone—some mathematicians seem to be interested only in numbers, for example—but it's true of many of us, probably most. I now believe the simplicity of investing everything in the single person of Jesus Christ is the whole secret of Bible-believing Christianity. Theoretically, Christianity teaches the Trinity, but God—what is God, really? A list of superlatives. The Holy Spirit? Technically, the Holy Spirit is a personality Who, along with the Father and the Son, can be worshiped, but for most Christians this spirit is little more than an abstraction cobbled together from seventeen references in the New Testament (none in the Old). But the Son, Jesus Christ? He's the Man-God who walked the earth and in some mysterious way resurrected Himself from the dead—"the greatest man who ever lived," a relative told me one time at Christmas, in a telltale understatement. Vreeland was right: it's people most of us are mostly interested in, and the religion that invested everything in one person—monotheism *personified*—is either a stroke of the shrewdest human genius or God's final truth.

Back in New York after the fateful trip to Houston, Blaine and I couldn't help noticing that the woman who lived next to the Rileys and who'd always been so careful with the condoms (if not with the window shades) was now expecting a baby. I, at least, had no explanation for that change of plans. The people on the other side of her who had entertained so often on the weekends quit doing so; no one ever came to visit now. With the basketball play-offs over, the single guy to the far right turned to the baseball games every night. Above him, the old man with the two white cockatoos, who never left his rooms and never had guests of any kind except the deliverymen with food-stuffs, kept putting out his homemade gruel for the pigeons, despite admonitions from the tenants' committee—public admonitions, naming him, in the monthly newsletter. Next to him, the lonely young woman was, if anything, even lonelier and ate even more chocolate. The naked computer hacker beneath her suddenly had a girlfriend in his life, who was also naked most of the time, even when they fought so viciously. Next to them the gay couple split up, and next to them the lonely bachelor was, if anything, even lonelier. The couple who'd been forced to bring the wife's aging mother into their small apartment was collapsing under the stress, and the pigeons were still nesting behind the curtains inside their neighbor's living room, coming and going by way of the ill-fitted casing for the air conditioner. (I finally told the concierge.) The fat man who sold sleazy paraphernalia over the Internet continued to make a killing, as did his neighbor, the salesman of medical supplies, with the help of his mobbed-up partner, with all hell just about to break loose when the salesman's wife finds out.

What a soap opera, and Blaine and I were

greedy for the juicy details (some of which I, but not Blaine, had to infer). Slowly but surely, the lives across the way blossomed into the litany of illustrated strivings and sufferings in *The Deity Next Door* that awaken in Blaine the profound compassion emblematic of any deity who'd be acceptable today. His omniscience of the mundane, as I think of it—inspired by and, in some implicit way, reflecting on all the detectives in the story—now comes to the fore. Blaine is the profoundest voyeur of our singular hearts and souls. The great Protestant theologian Dietrich Bonhoeffer wrote that we are all invited to participate in the suffering of God at the hands of a godless and suffering world. I needed to induce the reader to participate in the suffering of *Blaine*.

Officially, people come to Christ because of their sinful natures: confess these sins and acknowledge Christ as your Savior. In fact, however, many come to Christ out of suffering. Blaine has to understand this, but there hadn't been many Christians in the story to this point, and no down-home believers, the ones who really carry the water for the faith. Thus Blaine's fortuitous encounter with Brother Wayne in Times Square. A lot of these sidewalk preachers may be nuts, but Wayne definitely isn't. He's based on a young guy I knew in Dallas, a student at the Bible college. This real Wayne is perhaps the most transparently guileless individual I've ever met, and I felt rather strange listening to—recording—his testimony about his brutally painful divorce and ultimate reconciliation (a saga many times as long as the condensed version in *Deity*), but Wayne had no compunctions about telling it, because he believes people can learn from his story. In fact, every evangelical—of my acquaintance, at least—will be happy to tell you his or her Christian testimony, including private and embarrassing moments, in the hope that you'll understand that it is precisely the depth of suffering in the *broken* individual that calls forth the sustaining grace of Jesus.

One of the parts of Wayne's testimony that I omitted from *Deity,* because it was too long for my purposes, was about a special prayer. I want to add it here. After Wayne and his wife separated, she left for college and cut off all communication; after a good deal of trial and error, Wayne then learned about this prayer. "It's from the Book of Hosea, one of the minor prophets," he told me in Dallas years ago. "I don't think Hosea would appreciate that designation, but that's what we label him. When Hosea's wife Gomer was living in harlotry, God placed a hedge of thorns around her and prevented her lovers from having anything to do with her. And Gomer therefore came back to Hosea, who was using this story as an illustration of Israel's leaving God and then returning. According to the seminar I attended, there had been a lot of results from that prayer. So I began to pray for a hedge of thorns to be placed around my wife, for Satan to be bound, and for her to be miserable until she turned and began to seek the Lord, to see what He really wanted her to do. I started praying that prayer in March, but the divorce came through sometime in April. I kept on praying. I was hurting so bad, I wanted help so bad. I really felt I just couldn't bear all this. I was totally miserable, but really finally learning how to depend on the Lord. When a lot of people would say, 'Listen, it's no use, you're not going to get back together; it's over with, you might as well go find somebody else,' I knew that isn't God's way. God is a god of reconciliation. If I married someone else, according to Scripture, I'd be committing adultery. God's way is reconciliation. In Second Corinthians, He tells us He's given to us a ministry of reconciliation. The Bible is the backbone of everything I do. I knew that if I wanted to be happy I was going to have to do it God's way. I loved my wife more than anything and wanted her back and I tried to let her know. I wrote letters. My pastor and his wife even went up to her college to meet her and talk with her. That was not productive. I was living with my parents then, teaching some Sunday school, but doing very little preaching at all."

A couple of months after the divorce, Wayne received word through a friend that his now former wife wanted to see him. "I found myself sitting across from her in a restaurant," he told me. "This was the first time we had talked sociably in nine months. There was tension, though. It was so thick you could just about cut it. There were no smiles or friendly exchanges. I tried to be as gracious and kind as I could, sort of like a little puppy dog, wanting to work things out, but they didn't seem to be working out. Finally she said she didn't even know why she'd called me, we weren't going to get back together. But she did agree to let me come up the following Sunday for the whole day. She had heard some folks say that God would forgive me, which He will. I did come up on Saturday and we went shopping around the college. She went back to the dorm that afternoon and I stayed around, too, hoping she would come by, but she didn't. On Sunday morning I went to church. I recall very well when I left the church and returned to the hotel room I wept so hard I had to bury my face in the pillow because I was afraid the people in the next room would hear me. I seemed so close to getting her back, but not really. It was kind of like a bird that has flown away. You don't know whether it's going to come back or not.

"That was in June. It was some time before I heard anything else from her—maybe the last part of the summer. All this time I was still praying for the hedge of thorns. Consistently praying. Then I got word she wanted to see me again. I went up there and found out that she was having a really hard time, too. I could see her breaking, see her softening. She was also getting ready to leave school. It wasn't what she wanted. She was totally, totally miserable. Distraught."

Eighteen months after the divorce, Wayne

and his wife remarried. He told me in conclusion, "The greatest ministry we have in our lives—something we really enjoy doing—is talking with people who are going through the same thing we went through. We've been called by people we don't even know but have heard about us. 'My spouse has left me. What do I do?' But this testimony—this story, as you might call it—is something a lot of people don't know about. When we think back about it there's still pain there, it hurt so bad. It was some years before my wife was really able to talk to me about what she went through during those times, because it hurt her.

"So we've been down the road, and we've seen that God was faithful."

At some point in his life, Blaine had probably met truly pious individuals, but he'd never really engaged them. Not his fault, few in his world in New York have. If he'd encountered Wayne a year earlier—a year before the story in *Deity* begins—he'd have dismissed him as more proof that we humans can believe virtually anything; but now he has a different perspective, and now—in the novel—he's dealing with more than just *theology*. Wayne and his wife's pure faith put a whole new burden on the new deity: responsibility. God may appear to toy with the faithful—in the fashion, for example, that invites Job's complaints—but Jesus never did, and Blaine won't either.

In a book I highly recommend, *The God of the Philosophers,* the British philosopher Anthony Kenny asks whether it's ridiculous for agnostics to pray. In partial answer, Kenny asks a parallel question, whether it would be ridiculous for a sailor dismasted in the middle of the Atlantic to fire shots from his pistol, even though it's virtually impossible for these shots to be heard. No, it's not ridiculous, Kenny proposes, it's perfectly rational, just as it's rational for the spiritually lost human being who doesn't believe in the traditional Judeo-Christian God, yet feels the urge in moments of acute sympathy or suffering, to pray anyway. This is why my eighty-two-year-old father goes to a different church almost every Sunday in Houston, and my own father's search is why Blaine's father makes his unexpected entrance late in the story as the infirm old man who goes to a different church almost every Sunday.

Today, I wonder whether that disheartening situation with my father wasn't an almost unconscious factor in my motivation for writing this novel. At the very least, watching your father wither away in psychic agony—probably not too strong a phrase—isn't something you can just set aside, is it? I'll even admit that I've tried to coax him toward some formulation stronger than—more beneficial than—his favorite nostrums, that God is Nature, or Nature, God. Neither one seems to be doing him much good. But as a proud thinking man who rejected traditional faith decades earlier, he resists the implication behind my questions. But why are all those medications so acceptable instead? I don't follow the logic. Religion is a crutch? Among others. So be reasonable, Dad. Fire the pistol! Someone out there might be listening.

Sometimes I have nothing against pragmatism: First, do no harm. Second, is it working? Third, what is truth, anyway?*

Is the root cause of much of our suffering this fear of our own mortality? I know it's so with my father, and it might already be so with me, as I learned when I attended the funeral of the young son of one of the faculty members in Dallas. The text for the pastor's sermon that day was from Second Corinthians, the lovely passage in which Paul reminds that wayward congregation in that notoriously immoral city

---

*John 18:38—and only John. Matthew, Mark, and Luke omit Pontius Pilate's famous and important question.

that even if their earthly tent is torn asunder, they have a building from God, a house made not with their hands, but eternal in the heavens. So be of good courage, he reminds them, and walk by faith, for how preferable it is to be absent from the body and to be at home with the Lord.

The grieving father then stepped behind the pulpit. He was Luis Pantoja, and I tell this story with his permission. He spoke quietly of his son Luel's battle with cancer, of Luel's recent journey to the Holy Land, of how Luel had devoted what he knew would probably be the last year of his life to witnessing for the Lord. "The answer to our prayers is life," Luis Pantoja said of the Christian way, "and the answer to our prayers is death." He informed the audience that he was wearing his son's watch, because his son was now in a place where he wouldn't need it. It was midafternoon in Dallas, but Luis Pantoja said in closing, "Good mourning to you all."

There were no dry eyes in the church audi-
torium that afternoon—none except for Luis
Pantoja's, and I marveled at his composure
and courage. So did Paige Patterson, the president of the college, who now spoke briefly.
Paige told us that he had received permission
from the Pantoja family to proceed with the traditional conclusion of a Southern Baptist worship service, the invitation to accept Jesus Christ
as Lord and Savior. He asked for bowed heads
and closed eyes. I bowed my head and I closed
my eyes. He asked anyone who wanted to accept
Christ into his or her life to raise a hand.

"Only you and this minister will know of
this statement," he said, and I think he was
looking directly at me. Surely he was, if for no
other reason than I was probably the only person in the audience whom Paige knew to be
lost. (We had lots of conversations over the
course of that semester.)

"In a gathering this size," he continued,
"there must be a few who feel the need to make

this commitment." You'd think so, but I attended more than one church service in Dallas at which not a soul came forward. I was almost embarrassed for the preachers, but they get used to it. This afternoon, two people apparently raised their hands—and I came within a synapse of raising my own.

What happened must have been this: Luis Pantoja's marvelously courageous tribute to his son had, for me and, I assume, for many others present, struck at the heart of the problem. The world's demands are not mortised to fit neatly with our own needs; quite the contrary, it sometimes seems. We are fallen (to use the Christian terminology) and we do suffer and we do need help. In a vulnerable moment, I wanted *more* help, and what's the crime in that?

Time and again at the Bible college, believers told me they were born again only when they could slog no more through long days and longer nights of drinking, drugs, promiscuity, lying, guilt. Their sinful natures led them to the base of the cross. Perhaps, but I don't think this is the root psychology for most of us today, including believers. We in the West aren't into inner-directed sinfulness and guilt, and sometimes the Christian testimonies hardly bother with the sin and the guilt and proceed straight to the suffering and the mortality. We do see the sin, but we also see something else. *Gloria dei, vivens homo?* Yes, the glory of God is the living human being, but the guilt of God is the suffering human being.

Preachers are always reminding their congregations that it is Christians who fail Christianity, not vice versa, but some of their congregants don't buy it. Some of them—and a lot of nonchurchgoers—are just angry with God, bottom line. He seems so far, far away and the Fall so long, long ago. That Fall may have been willful sinning for Adam and Eve, but it's unwarranted inheritance for you and me, and as such isn't sin but suffering. Angry people do feel this way. Atone? *You* atone, God. You started it all.

It was my friend Paul P., the student of comparative religions, who pointed out that this unfolding scene in Blaine's apartment building has many parallels with Nathanael West's *Miss Lonelyhearts,* in which the author of the Lonelyhearts column in the local newspaper becomes so mired in the pain of his correspondents he falls into delusion and despair. I had read the novel, of course, but many years earlier; I should have made the connection for myself, but hadn't. In an e-mail Paul concluded, "West's book is a brilliant portrait of the fate of the messianic impulse in a complex culture that no longer has the resources to address human suffering."

Just so, and the feeling of divine responsibility begins to overwhelm the new messiah on West Twenty-fourth Street. Blaine can't tolerate the anguish of the writer, not so young anymore, who's almost evicted for nonpayment and remains on the edge from month to month, surviving on plastic as she cranks out proposal after proposal for the magazines, landing only the occasional poorly paid service piece. The actress with whom this writer is friends, with whom she often shares a dinner of rice and salad, who struggles through her auditions, no longer able to summon the right emotions for the roles—her failing career overwhelms Blaine's own emotions. He could save these two women, could he not, somehow?! The temptation is agony, and the sudden suicide of the actress and the collapse into despair of the writer are the last straws. The wages of sin may be death but the gift of suffering is eternal life through . . . Blaine, who is monotheism re-personified. Within a matter of just five pages, he precipitously loses his way in this fallen world. Confronted with his wife's questions, he's mute, and Melanie (her marriage now a vise) loses her way as well. You know the rest.

Many, many times I've been asked whether I'd known from the beginning that the story in *Deity* would lead to this pivotal moment of the messiah's disintegrating marriage, or did I change my mind as I was writing? If I changed my mind, did I think about going back and writing the marriage out of the story in the first place? Yes, I did change my mind. In the beginning, I liked the idea of the married messiah— the Protestant messiah—for the sake of something different, if nothing else, but we'll agree that Melanie is a shadowy figure in the story, more or less restricted to domestic duties, somewhat more delineated than Mary and Martha in the Gospels, but not much. I did write what would have been an important scene in which Blaine finally tells Melanie what's going on, and Melanie, who isn't religious, isn't impressed. In fact, she's offended by his claim to have saved the life of their child. Certainly I could have used this complication to spin out all kinds of twists for the plot, but I could never make myself believe it. So Blaine never tells her. She's a shadowy presence in *Deity* because she's a shadowy presence for Blaine.

I was as surprised as everyone by the latest development in the story—it took less than a morning to write—and I wasn't happy about it, but what choice did I have, when you stop to consider? There is, in the makeup of any messiah, along with the profound compassion, the countervailing element of the rogue male. We find this with Jesus in the Gospels, that's for sure, when he tells a scribe that foxes have holes, and birds of the air have nests, but the Son of Man has nowhere to lay his head. We find it when he brusquely tells a disciple, who requests permission to leave for a few days in order to bury his father, to stay where he is and leave the dead to bury their own dead.[*] That's cold, and after that morning at my desk we find a bit of the rogue male in the makeup of Blaine. However, I didn't want to go back and write Melanie out of the story. I think this modern cataclysm plays well in the life of this modern messiah.

Now everything comes together as it comes apart for Blaine. The realization—the transformation—the epiphany—is complete. We've moved from the first sentence in which Blaine has no idea that he's divine to a Blaine who's so divine he feels literally all alone. He finally knows in his own heart and soul what we've known since the last clause of the first sentence of his story. Faith in a fact—that's what knowing is, right? Now Blaine has the confidence of his predecessor, and there's a divine spring in his step. Everything else is beside the point,

*Matthew 8:20–22; Luke 9:58–60.

including the long interview with the Catholic-oriented psychiatrist set up by Father Harris. (I'm gratified that readers become as infuriated as I am by that dork's blithering incompetence, by his inability to take off the mask and react like a real, live human being when his desk is suddenly hovering about a foot off the floor and his prized Tiffany lamp is teetering in jeopardy—an important scene, it would seem, because it's the one main instance in which Blaine succumbs to the temptation to show off (the first scene with Father Harris wasn't showing off, per se), but it was really just cheap payback on my part for all the lame interviews I endured for my ill-fated oral history, *Shrinks: They Do the Talking, We Listen.*)

But now what? What's Blaine called to do? He's conquered his own unbelief, but how does he conquer the world's? In the temptation scene in the wilderness, Jesus tells Satan not to put the Lord your God to the test. Easy for him to say, but what about Blaine today? Even the Jews of Galilee were always seeking signs and proof, and Jesus did sometimes accede to their wishes, so how can Blaine possibly proceed without providing such signs and proof for today's audience? He needs to levitate the largest lamp the world has ever seen. Or does he? With one set of doubts put to rest, this new set consumes him as he patrols the streets of Manhattan, for the most part staying with friends who try to be understanding without understanding a thing, but sometimes bunking at the modest residential hotel on Forty-third Street, admonishing some of the sinful, accomplishing numerous small miracles, waiting for the main chance.

But not preaching. I'm still amazed that I've never been asked, not once, why Blaine doesn't do any official preaching. People are concerned about the lack of praying, but you don't miss the preaching. Interesting. Even though if you open any red-letter edition of the

Bible and rifle the pages of the four Gospels, there's a lot of red ink. The irony is that I had my answer ready to go: What's Blaine got to preach about? What's his mission? What's his message? He may admonish some of the sinful, but his instincts are essentially humanistic, not sectarian. Moreover, redemption has already been offered by Jesus Christ. Blaine definitely seems to be *of* the Christian tradition, but what's left for him to do *within* it? He doesn't seem to be fulfilling an ordained destiny, so he needs to be creating one, somehow.

By the way, this is where I initially placed the scene in the psychiatric hospital that I referred to early in this afterword, in the context of the psychiatrist's story about the woman who committed suicide—the reference that should have puzzled you, because you'd just finished the novel and didn't remember any psychiatric hospital and were wondering how you could have forgotten so soon. You hadn't. I was just playing around. I cut that scene, by far the most significant of all the cuts from the manuscript, which were many, because the early drafts were half again as long as the published book. In the interim, I'd reread *Mariette in Ecstasy* and realized that, everything else being equal, lots of language requires lots of talent; less language, less (speaking only of prose now, not poetry). This isn't to say that Ron Hansen isn't a terrific writer. He is, but I'm sure he'd agree that as difficult as his 179-page novel was to write, the 400-page version would have been exponentially more challenging, and perhaps just not doable today. Both the genius and the conviction—there's the rub—are required; a veritable Dostoyevsky is required. If any critic were inspired toward such flattery (which none turned out to be), I wanted to be compared with Mark, by far the briefest of the four gospelists, not with verbose Matthew.

I couldn't handle the bigger book, which got better with every cut. However, the psychiatric hospital was a tough call, because the scene worked so well to remind us that just as our contemporary context probably trumps any possible miracle, so it probably trumps any claim to—even the *fact* of—divinity. In that discarded scene, Blaine is visiting his and Melanie's friend Stephanie, whose story is pretty much the same as the story from *Shrinks: They Do the Talking, We Listen* about the woman who finally took the overdose in the hotel room. Sitting in the ward, Blaine wonders if he could cure this profoundly troubled woman. If her illness is strictly a chemical-electrical-physiological problem with the wiring, of course he could, but what if it's a sickness of her imma-terial, perhaps immortal soul? This probably gets more complicated. While this quandary unfolds, the setting of the scene implicitly brings up the question of Blaine's own sanity. There has been absolutely no implication that he's been crazy all along—we know this is not the case—but we also understand that, should the time come, he'll nevertheless be judged in the same categories and jargon of mental health as Stephanie is being judged. "Delusions of grandeur" and "paranoia" are official symptoms in the DSM-IV; "divinity" isn't.

Chapter Four

T HE TENET OF inerrancy declares that every word of the Bible is divinely inspired and therefore theologically, philosophically, scientifically, and historically true, as the recitation goes. In my experience, almost everyone snickers when first introduced to this ultraconservative provocation, then they become intrigued for the same reason I did at the Bible college in Dallas, Blaine does at his desk in New York, and (I hope) you do during the scene with Father Harris in the restaurant: it's not really a snickering matter. One quick and obvious example: Jesus raises Lazarus from the dead only in the Gospel of

John. Why would Matthew, Mark, and Luke omit this most important of all Jesus's miracles? If all three men wrote their gospels years, if not decades, before John wrote his, as most commentators believe, how did they miss the story but John get it? Let the debate continue, but one plausible explanation is that the other three writers didn't know about it, because it wasn't part of the oral tradition, because nothing remotely like it ever happened. But inerrancy helps save the day for the believer.

Remember the famously inopportune remarks of Jerry Falwell and Pat Robertson shortly after September 11 to the effect that God may have withdrawn his divine protection from America and set us up, presumably because either His will and our enemy's prayers were aligned in this one instance, or (the more complex situation, theologically) because He and Allah were in cahoots? Everyone hooted in derision, but in order to do so they had to ignore the clear testimony of inerrant, divinely inspired Scripture: Jesus said that the hairs on your head are numbered, that not a sparrow falls but for the knowledge of God.* (In the Koran, it's the welfare of the ant that warrants the full attention of Allah.†) If an omniscient, omnipotent God did create our universe, He must by definition know everything that will ever happen, or He's not omniscient, and He must in some way cause everything to happen, or at least allow it, or He's not omnipotent. Through his spokesman, Ari Fleischer, George W. Bush denounced the Falwell and Robertson statements, but as a Bible-believing Christian whose favorite political figure is so famously Jesus, our president probably privately agrees with those two supporters. Such Christians can't—or shouldn't—expect any contradiction between God's omniscience and His omnipotence. Every role of the dice is envi-

---

*Matthew 10:29–30; Luke 12:6.

†This is the metaphorical gloss on sura 27, "The Ants," v. 18–19.

sioned, if not ordained: Providence reigns. (Exactly how this view of God's Providence allows room for efficacious prayers is complicated.) I've also read that Bush, Falwell, and Robertson also agree that God played favorites in Florida because He knew what was coming and wanted the better Christian in the White House to exact our just revenge. Now, why would God sanction both the attack and the revenge? That one I can't answer. You'll have to ask Him, or them.

Maybe that last paragraph is a little glib and self-serving, but the doctrine of inerrancy really is germane for establishing or casting doubt on the divinity of Jesus, and therefore it may be germane regarding Blaine's own standing. In any event, he's convinced of this, he's the one who counts, and this is what he's trying to make Father Harris understand in the restaurant. He also probably knows more about this subject than his friend the priest does, because, generally speaking, Catholics, even conservative

Catholics, aren't nearly as obsessed about inerrancy as their counterpart Protestants. (Protestants may boast that theirs is the unmediated encounter with the Almighty, but in fact their Bible serves as the rock on which their faith is founded. The truly unmediated encounter would be the one in which the supplicant burns his chosen Scripture to a crisp, incinerates his cash, his car, and his clothes, spurns his family (as Jesus instructed his disciples to do*), flees to the desert, and throws himself on the altar of utter ignorance and screams at the top of his lungs, I don't have or know a goddamn thing, God, including you! Now *that* is an unmediated encounter with the Almighty—until they start feeding you the meds in the psych ward.)

With Blaine, who's divine but unchurched, defending the doctrine of inerrancy, if only for the sake of the argument, against Father Har-

---

*Matthew 10:34–37.

ris, who's not divine but very much Churched, my hope was that the intrigue of these role reversals would play against and sustain the exposition—that and the grand meal itself, culminating in Father Harris's eventual realization that he's been eating a lot of the excellent bread and drinking a lot of fine Chianti even though he hasn't asked the waiter for more of either. I love the bit when Harris abruptly pauses with the wineglass at his lips, glances at the bottle, which is still half full though he alone has had four or five glasses, and then looks carefully at Blaine, who returns the gaze in perfect innocence. More wine, Father?

For some reason, nevertheless, this restaurant scene doesn't have the impact I've always thought it should. One addition that would have helped is the Ascension, because it's a good story and it would have been a good test of where Father Harris and the reader stand as strict constructionists. Belatedly, I'll tell you about it now. In this post-Resurrection appearance at Emmaus, as described by Luke in Acts, Christ charges his disciples to witness for the faith in all Judea and Samaria and to the ends of the earth. Then he's lifted up onto a cloud, which spirits him out of sight. Clearly, this passage is weighty with theological significance. It's the kind of direct description we don't have for the Resurrection itself, so it makes us confront the big question head-on: did Luke and his contemporaries really believe that Christ rose up into outer space, from where he now looks down, or was Luke simply invoking as a metaphor the imagery of the heavens-above universe which was the accepted worldview at the time? More important, was this event the subjective, mystical experience of believers only, proof of the presence within them of the Holy Spirit, or was it a public event in the material world? Could you have recorded the Ascension on your videocam? I wish Blaine had asked Father Harris. I wish he'd asked him if the lamp had really risen from his desk when they met the first time, or had this event been just the mystical experience of a man overwhelmed by the divine presence?

My evangelical friends who believe there's no contradiction of any kind between the Jesus of the material world and the Christ of faith necessarily answer that, yes, they could have recorded the Ascension (if not the lamp) with their videocams, but I think Father Harris would have answered "no" regarding the Ascension and "no comment" regarding the lamp, even though he had good reason to believe that the episode was exactly what Blaine claimed it was, a minor miracle. Knowing the percentage of sales of *The Deity Next Door* generated by regular bookstores (including Amazon) versus Christian bookstores, assuming that the large majority of the regular-store readers dismiss inerrancy as absurd, while a considerable portion of the Christian-store readers accept the doctrine, I judge that about 80 percent of my readers do *not* believe they could have recorded the Ascension—or the Resurrection, for that matter—on their videocams.

Fair enough, but then why do all of you naysayers believe that the lamp really did lift off Father Harris's desk, and that Blaine really did cure Timothy and the other boy of their cancers? *Deity* is a commercial novel written by a rank amateur, but as you're reading the story you believe it, by all reports; the Gospels proclaim themselves to be inspired by God, they are the basis of one of the dominant religious faiths on Earth, but as you read them you doubt many of the stories, by all reports. Why is this? I was just trying to create a little confusion in your minds.

Without the acceptance of inerrancy, how do Father Harris and other serious Christians know if a biblical passage or doctrine is given by God or manufactured by man? It's been a long time since Harris was in school, and he's surprised to realize that this question as framed by Blaine isn't utterly ridiculous. His interlocutor presses the rhetorical advantage. If you, as a Christian, accept the Resurrection of Jesus Christ—the most supernatural event in all of history—what's your problem with accepting all the lesser miracles? Harris hesitates again. Does he see the dominoes falling? If you want Christ's Resurrection to attest to all the subsequent theology—pretty much the definition of the faith—don't you logically have to let it attest to the other miraculous episodes in the Bible that present that theology? I wanted the payoff for Blaine's argument to be clear but not explicit: either the endorsement of Jesus does indeed give the benefit of the doubt to the ancient stories, including the ones in the Old Testament, or the testimony of Jesus and the other worthies regarding those fabulous stories backfires and casts doubt on their own credentials for divinity or sainthood, as the case may be.

I mentioned earlier that one of my modest

motives for *Deity* was enticing everyone to think afresh about the concept of divinity. As a thoughtful deity, Blaine has to think afresh, too. Should his own divinity settle all doubts about the divinity of Jesus? This seems to put the cart *way* before the horse in some strange way, but Father Harris lacks a ready answer to this provocation, other than the fact that he's never doubted the divinity of Jesus Christ. Does Blaine's divinity prove that Moses really did part the waters of the Red Sea? If so, this could be a problem, because Blaine himself isn't inclined to put much stock in those Old Testament tales. And does it follow from Blaine's apparently Christian divinity that all the other religions are wrong after all? One problem with the scene is that this question is only hinted at, but if the answer is yes, well, Blaine has always been uncomfortable with all the exclusionary claims to truth in the Bible, and all the war-like proclamations. Specifically, is Blaine proof positive that Islam is a false religion? If so, real trouble. As Blaine has learned while dabbling in the Koran, many devout Muslims make an assertion of inerrancy for their chosen Scripture, and no one likes to be wrong about his religion.

Blaine and I applaud ecumenism at every opportunity as a compromise required for the sake of comity, in the manner in which we tell the other man that his wife is pretty and his kids are smart as well as cute (Mencken), but let's at least acknowledge the unspoken but indisputable contradiction at the very heart of ecumenism: every theistic faith of real substance requires the repudiation of every other theistic faith of a *different* real substance; for any such faith of mine to be right, yours has to be wrong; a tolerant theistic faith is, at its roots, a vitiated faith. This is true even within the Judeo-Christian tradition. Remember when the pope remarked before a microphone some years ago that the visitation of the Holy Spirit at Pentecost marked "the new and everlasting covenant," and he got into trouble with Israel? He had inadvertently broken the tacit agreement of ecumenism, but he has to believe this about the Pentecost, as the Jews well know. He's the pope! (Earlier this year—2002—his house theologian, Cardinal Ratzinger, issued a document acknowledging the validity of the Jews' anticipation of the messiah. The main difference, the cardinal wrote, is that the Jews are waiting for the First Coming, Christians for the Second. Now that's more like it: classic ecumenism, 210 pages worth.)

As for those easily ecumenical Christians who have no problem at all with the idea that their faith is just *their* faith, no more, the aphorist E. M. Cioran had the final word. Such fair-minded faith, he declared with deadly accuracy, no longer has the energy to be intolerant. This is where most of us in the West are today, and when confronted with a faith that does still generate the energies of intolerance, we're justifiably dumbstruck and outraged.

Can we even afford our chosen religions now, or would we be better off without them? It's conceivable that Blaine is bad news for the world.

In Blaine's field, the main chance is in the Holy Land, or at least it has to go through there, but I was at a loss for the plot device that would accomplish this for him before a writer friend told me about Edgar Rice Burroughs's solution to an equivalent narrative dilemma in *Tarzan of the Apes*—or maybe it was one of the other Tarzan novels. Anyway, after Tarzan has fallen into a deep pit without hope of escape at the end of one chapter, the next chapter begins, more or less, "After Tarzan escaped from the pit . . ." Simple as that, he got out! Once you know about this tried-and-true literary non sequitur, you start seeing the equivalent device used by all kinds of writers, and if the story is strong enough they can get away with it. I guess I did: suddenly Blaine is in the Holy Land and deeply moved by his entry into Jerusalem, as every visitor is, especially every visitor with some sense of coming home. Blaine is riding not on a donkey but in a van, and greeted not with the hosannas of his followers but rudely by the service-industry personnel he encounters, but the famous light off the limestone of the old city really is incomparable, and Nietzsche himself would have appreciated the power of the place to shake the soul.

In my experience, the only comparable venue is the Big Island in Hawaii. Is the lava desert on the leeward coastline the most intimidating setting anywhere for a famed resort destination? I think it must be. All the Bay Area money now pouring in will eventually ruin this island, but give these arrivistes some credit: at least they pick up the fact that this liquid land has all the power, the mojo, the beneficial con-

fluences, the superior vortices, the good vibra-
tions. Even the residents on the other islands
will admit as much. Standing on these lava
flows at the edge of the Pacific Ocean, braced
against the howling trade winds, gazing
around at the display of ancient volcanic peaks
in the high distance, the pope of Rome himself
would have to acknowledge the force field ema-
nating from these volcanoes, presided over by
the goddess Pele. I'm not at all surprised that
post offices, hotels, and the Hawaii Volcanoes
National Park receive, every year, hundreds of
boxes loaded with lava rocks from tourists who
took them home despite warnings that Pele
would take insult, who were then beset with
inordinately bad luck or fortune, and who now
want to set things right. A good friend tried
this years ago, mailing boxes of pilfered rocks
to her estranged husband who was vacationing
on Kauai, who then deposited them along the
Pali Coast of that island, but it was too late to
save that marriage. You couldn't pay me to

take one of these rocks off-island; I'd sooner deal in the local homegrown.

I'm totally hooked on the Big Island and on Jerusalem, where it's no surprise to me that hundreds of visitors are afflicted with the Jerusalem syndrome, and this is why Blaine, pretending to be one of them, joins the group therapy session under the auspices of one of the Christian foundations. For a while I wondered whether this scene was too clever for its own good—an actual messiah pretending to be a messiah in order to learn more about the distinction—but the scene seems to work, so it stayed. Maybe it works because it's the only remotely humorous scene in the whole novel. There's not another intentional laugh anywhere (just as there's no openhearted laughter in the Bible; it's always directed with mocking intent). Plus I've always been intrigued by the fact that we humans can believe something while knowing that it's not true. (Reading a novel is the most pertinent case in point.) In this group session, the young guy from Massachusetts, Peter, knows he can't possibly be the Son of God but nevertheless feels that he is. He doesn't state this diagnosis in so many words, but the point is clear: Peter is knowingly delusional. Blaine is, by now, at last, totally confident of his own divinity, but who wouldn't pause when confronted with such a syndrome, so I don't find it at all surprising when he reacts somewhat defensively and turns back the clock on the wall, literally, just to show everyone in the room a thing or two. What could be richer than the rejection of such incontrovertible evidence of Blaine's powers by this bunch of delusionals?

But then, a dozen pages later, we're at one of the most somber sites on Earth, the Church of the Holy Sepulchre, the birthplace of the Christian faith. On no scene in *Deity* did I work harder (while omitting certain damning details, like the Eastern Orthodox priest on duty with his hand out for tribute), and for good reason. Did the Buddha die for his people? Did Muhammad? Did the Buddha rise from his tomb? Did Muhammad? No, so if in fact Jesus was resurrected from the dead, the truth claim of Christianity is confirmed, it is the one true religion, Christians are justified in their world-wide evangelizing, Muslims and the believers of all other faiths are dead wrong. Paul could not have been more clear in his First Epistle to the Corinthians: if Christ hasn't been raised from the dead, we haven't been redeemed and our faith is worthless; without the Resurrection of the Savior, Paul wrote, the very idea of the "Savior" is a cruel hoax. Or do you think Paul got it wrong?

The problem here is that just *believing* Jesus rose from the dead isn't enough, not nearly enough, because people can and do believe anything. If mere belief is the only criterion, any competing faith is a true one. Only *knowing* that the Resurrection actually happened as an event in the physical world proves that this is the one case in which divinity is not simply an assertion. This is why Bible-believing Christians are adamant about the proven historicity of the Resurrection that happened right here, at this sepulchre in the rotunda of this ancient church in the middle of the Old City. By definition, the questions surrounding the historical, bodily Resurrection of Jesus Christ are the most profound and important of them all, and I hope the stately cadences of the sentences in this scene reflect this fact.

Hard as it is to remember now, when I was working on *Deity* the Oslo accords were being held, Bill Clinton's initiatives had the momentum, and it looked as if the Palestinians and the Israelis might actually make peace. But it wasn't in the cards, not really, and never had been. Blaine knows this, and he also knows that he should be able to do better. As a divine messiah standing before the Wailing Wall, he feels he should be able to—but I was not and still am not so sure, because one classic Christological problem that has always bothered me is whether Jesus Christ was *as divine as* God in terms of omniscience and omnipotence. (For the sake of this question, grant the divinity.) Would Jesus, like God, have had foreknowledge of the attack on the Pentagon and the Twin Towers, for example? But forget the conditional with Jesus. Blaine is here and now. *Does* Blaine share this foreknowledge with God? I'm glad my novel preceded the attack.

Just as Blaine feels he should be able to bring peace to the Holy Land but doesn't, so God could have prevented the Holocaust but didn't, and every believer is left with the fallout from this most famous example of God's most famous Silence (which deserves the honorific capitalization in my book). So now the subject is theodicy—the problem of God's relations with mankind, popularly known by its most problematic element, the problem of evil. My toughest assignment here was nailing Blaine's frame of mind and spirit as he flies home to

America in his own silence. Is there any guilt in his mind at all for not bringing peace to Palestine? What about in God's mind? Or is it foolish to even speak in terms of God's mind, about which we can't possibly understand a single thing? Do we really have any idea what we're even talking about when we throw around words like omniscience and omnipotence? Is God responsible for everything? Does He have responsibility to fulfill *our* list of superlatives and obligations for Him? Who are we to judge? Is our kind of caring His kind of caring? Does He have His own definition of tough love? Does He have any moral responsibility to us at all? Who said?

In the end, I decided to let the questions fill Blaine's mind and then to let his own silence speak for itself, as God's Silence speaks so eloquently for itself. (Readers have asked if this was an authorial cop-out. I think not. If there's any cop-out, it's not mine.) For the first time, I've just counted the list of these and the other rhetorical questions that conclude the Holy Land chapter. I knew this interrogation was a long one, but twenty-two questions in all? No wonder it's the most quoted passage from the book.

One night a friend at my apartment for dinner asked what's supposed to happen in the real Second Coming. What a sickening feeling that was. Believe it or not, I hadn't even thought about this. I've admitted that I didn't worry in the beginning about exactly what kind of deity or messiah I was writing about, and even when it became clear to Blaine and me that he was a Christian incarnation of some sort, I still didn't give a thought to the pertinent biblical passages about the official Second Coming. I was thinking about a next messiah whose career begins quietly and slowly picks up speed. I wasn't sure how it was going to end. But what if the real Second Coming put constraints on what I could plausibly do in *Deity*? After everyone left I asked my wife to do the dishes while I rushed off to do my homework.

As I knew it would, the *Ryrie Study Bible* led me immediately to the first important passage, and I guess I should cite in its entirety this vital declaration from Jesus, Matthew 24:29–31:

But immediately after the tribulation of those days, the sun will be darkened, and the moon will not give its light, and the stars will fall from the sky, and the powers of heaven will be shaken, and then the sign of the Son of Man will appear in the sky, and then all the tribes of the earth will mourn, and they will see the Son of Man coming on the clouds of the sky with power and great glory. And He will send forth His angels with a great trumpet and they will gather

*together His elect from the four winds, from one
end of the earth to another.*

One passage in Acts and then two in Revelation depict the same scene in similar language. All were sobering reading indeed for
me, because if Blaine is going to work out his
destiny in the Christian tradition, how in the
world could I jibe his story-in-progress with
these biblical passages? True, most readers
wouldn't know anything about them, but my
serious Christian friends certainly would, and
I would. How could I get around the fact that
the Bible calls for Jesus Christ to come roaring
down from heaven on a cloud the next time?
And what about the fact that the Second Coming is just that, the second coming of the same
Christ, not a new messiah, not a next messiah,
but the same messiah for a second and final
time of judgment? Looking back, it's incredible
that I'd so naively dismissed or overlooked this

problem—but it's a good thing I did, because its difficulty might have stopped me cold in the earliest days of the work. As it was, I now had much too much invested to just throw in the towel, and I endured the longest eight hours of my life before I came up with the simple and, I still believe, correct rationalization for my concept: the dramatic, apocalyptic Second Coming that didn't work for my purposes in the novel doesn't work for our purposes, either—the culture's at large, I mean. It doesn't even work for the churchgoing public, most of whom don't really expect the sky to open when the time finally comes, if it ever does. You can check this out for yourself with a poll at the door on Sunday morning.

Nevertheless, to assure knowledgeable readers that I knew what I was talking about, that I hadn't simply overlooked the damaging contradiction at the heart of my story, I had to go back and have Father Harris confront Blaine with the pertinent biblical passages so that Blaine could ask in reply, But do you really think Christ will ride down from the sky next time? Of course Harris doesn't believe this, as implied by his extended silence. Nor has a single reader ever complained to me about the contradiction between the Bible's Second Coming and my own version of events. And you know why? We like Blaine. We're rooting for him. With the busted marriage and the rest of it, he's one of us—but uniquely so. (Ironically, it was the out-moded image of the sky-rending Second Coming that provided my first working title for the novel, *The Sky Next Time.* In fact, that title held until just a few months before publication—it was even the title in the publisher's catalogue— when I changed it over the almost dead body of my agent, Joe S., who derides the hokey *The Deity Next Door* to this day, though he acknowl-edges that it's working pretty well.)

The extravagantly public displays, includ-ing bringing peace to the Holy Land, that Blaine could have used for the proclamation of his deity in his *First* Coming, should it have come to that in the end, were the most enjoyable writing of all for me. Of course, the story doesn't come to that in the end, so none of these scenes are in the book, alas. I still like them, however, and I spent a lot of time on them, and this is my chance to identify my favorites. One subset of such feats featured Blaine fiddling with some key factor in the makeup of the physical universe, like slightly altering the speed of light, or slowing down the atomic clock at the Naval Observatory by a millionth of a second, or changing the 160th place to the right of the decimal in pi. All very clever, but not visual enough. How could they be shown on TV? Besides, it's an open question whether God has the power to alter the numerical values, equations, and algorithms that describe and power the world He Himself created. I can see how infusing a dead body with the spark of life might be easier than changing the Pythagorean theorem—and this theorem is as simple as they come.

Better—safer—was having Blaine take over the CNN satellites, *Atlas Shrugged* style, but my favorite idea of all was having him call a major news conference at a little-used military base in Iowa and then having an out-of-commission, rusting, and pilotless airplane taxi out of the knee-high grass onto the landing strip, take off, fly around the field a couple of times, land perfectly, and taxi back to its parking place. Pretty impressive right there, but the real kicker is the eerie silence, because the engines on the plane aren't running. All hell breaks loose, but what's most important is what does *not* happen: people do *not* prostrate themselves before the new messiah. This was my critical new understanding about Blaine's story, and it carried into the Transfiguration scene set in Arizona as part of Blaine's road trip out West. In the Synoptic Gospels, the actual Transfiguration of Jesus into a glowing apparition of holiness takes place on a high mountaintop in the company of Peter, James, and John—the key disciples—but I'd worked on a scene in which Blaine provocatively strides the fairways of one of the great golf resorts, his face shining like the sun, his garments white as light. But for the life of me I couldn't imagine the right reaction from the plaided hackers in their golf carts. They'd be dumbstruck, certainly, but would they put two and two together when confronted with Blaine's proclamation of his deity? I doubted it. Would anything put the folks on their knees today? This becomes maybe *the* issue at the heart of *The Deity Next Door,* in my opinion, and it's the question I recommend for discussion by all the book clubs that have taken up the text. Would anything put all of us seriously on our knees today? I'll believe such an expression of awe and faith when I see it, and I don't expect to, as I realized while working on this modified Transfiguration scene, and then on the airport scene. The people on the golf course and at the airfield, despite what they've just incontrovertibly witnessed, would not declare themselves followers of this messiah. They just wouldn't—definitely not the Hindus and Muslims among them, probably not the nominal Christians, maybe not even the evangelicals—so I moved the Transfiguration scene from the golf course to the privacy of the desert cul-de-sac where Blaine encounters the colorful and dusty old hermit (the closest to a disciple he ever has), and I cut the airfield scene entirely. Blaine's story heads precipitously in a different direction.

Following the real Transfiguration in the Gospels, God's voice issues from a bright cloud and declares to Peter, James, and John that He is well pleased with His beloved Son, to Whom they should listen. I didn't want any such business in *Deity,* which is why this part of the Transfiguration is missing from my version. In fact, God makes no appearance in this novel at all, as only a couple of you have noticed (or, in any event, commented on). Two reasons. First, the story is about Blaine and *us,* in its essence, not about Him; in this matter, too, I wanted His Silence to speak for itself. Second, and this may sound strange, given what some have described as the blasphemy of my basic project, I thought bringing in God as an actual "character" would be, well, blasphemous. Perhaps this timidity is a lopsided nod toward the logic of Blaise Pascal's wager—not to be confused with his law, which states that the pressure applied to a confined fluid is transmitted equally throughout that fluid in all directions. This phenomenon is the basis of hydraulics, and though Pascal is often thought of as the earliest Christian existentialist, his famous wager is just as calculating as his science, suggesting that if Christianity is false, nothing of importance has been lost by adhering to it anyway, while if it's true, every-

thing is lost by rejecting it. Christians sometimes use this logic (though not explicitly) to
explain their passion for evangelizing: if their
faith is false, they may have misled people but
they won't be held accountable in the end,
while if it's true, they'll be held accountable for
their failure to evangelize. But surely genuine
faith must issue from some motivation beyond
such cold-blooded shrewdness! Of course, the
same objection could be put forward about a
faith born in extremis, such as my father's
would be, but I don't see such a faith as calcu-
lated. I see it as gushing forth from need, and
if I were God, I'd reject the wagered prayer but
welcome the truly needy man's. But with this
assessment I'm assuming that faith is an all-
or-nothing proposition, and nothing could be
further from the truth. Every Christian I know
will acknowledge moments of doubt. Given the
radical nature of the basic proposition, the
Silence, the delayed Second Coming, and other

factors, who wouldn't wonder? It may well be that God takes what he can get, and Blaine will certainly have to.

During one of our many discussions about the plot of *Deity,* my agent, born a Jew, baptized in Rome, now a practicing Buddhist after his own fashion, proposed that whatever else happens in the story, we have to crucify this messiah, too, just as we did the first one. Absolutely right, Joe S. If the large majority of Jewish believers weren't ready for Christ two thousand years ago, certainly we—Jews, Christians, and all the rest—aren't ready for Blaine today. (Definitely not "all the rest.") Even in the Judeo-Christian West, we're heading at warp speed in other directions. Many of us may want to believe, but we don't believe, and there's nothing we can do about it—except wait until the wheel turns again, which it might, for whatever reason, who knows? Maybe God is taking, or will take, a different direction, too, I don't care what the hard-liners say about His immutable nature. The radical and much-hashed-over differences between His recorded behavior in the Old and New Testaments augur well for this possibility; this view of God even has an official name, process theology. In Dallas, I was intrigued by this and all the other left-wing notions about the *invisible* church, *implicit* faith, *anonymous* Christians, *religionless* Christianity, *liberation* theology, and, best of all, Christocentric *atheism*. There's really no end to the revisionist doctrines dreamed up by well-meaning theologians in the cause of preserving something—anything—that can be called Christian faith and lived authentically, while setting aside the old paradigms and "faith structures" that simply don't square with their best knowledge of God's creation. These thinkers claim to be preserving authentic Christianity, not denigrating it; they believe that a Christ for our times must be more than a revived corpse. Of course, they might as well label their books and essays "For Professional Use Only," but these are important concepts for my story, and I decided that as good an opportunity as any to introduce them in *Deity* would be Blaine's encounter with the Christian bikers in Moab, and the ride with them down Highway 191 to Blanding. (A number of readers have wondered about any analogy in my mind between these bearded bikers, the only bearded characters in *Deity,* and Jesus's disciples—some rough analogy, maybe—but, to my surprise, no one has questioned whether Blaine would really ride a Harley in the first place. This seems to be accepted easily, I guess because it fits with the stereotype of the rogue male. For the same reason, I don't think it's much of a stretch to picture Jesus on a hog.) My aim for this scene was modest in the beginning, but now I think that the leader of those bikers,

Jazz (in my mind, always a Dennis Hopper look-alike, except for skin color), is one of the more important supporting characters in the novel. He makes only this one appearance, but he's such a great guy—modeled after a biker and motorcycle mechanic I knew in Austin in the sixties, a guy whose quality was manifest to me from the first moment. Blaine has the same reaction to Jazz, and I hope the point is clear to everyone: Blaine is divine, and that's great, but Jazz is superior as only a human can be, because for us it's not so easy.

Among theologians, Cambridge philosopher John Wisdom's parable of the gardener is famous, and justly so, because it goes to the heart of the matter today as keenly as some of Jesus's parables resonated with his audiences. When the bikers are forced off the highway by high winds and take shelter at the abandoned gas station, the discussion into which Jazz entices Blaine as they look at the untidy desert garden behind the station is actually a modified version of the Wisdom parable, which starts with two visitors finding some isolated vigorous plants in an otherwise rather neglected environment. This doesn't appear to be a well-kept garden, and no one in the neighborhood has ever seen a gardener on the job; they've heard reports, that's all. Still, one of the two visitors insists that a gardener has been coming, perhaps at night. The other visitor says no, any gardener would be looking after the whole place, not just isolated plants. As they continue to tour the garden, the two visitors find more signs that might indicate the care of a gardener, but also more signs that cast doubt, and there are even some signs that a person of malicious intent may have been here. In the end, the one visitor still insists that a benevolent gardener is coming to look after the thriving plants, while the other observer still says no.

Blaine catches on, of course. The diametrically opposed beliefs of the two visitors are based on exactly the same observations. The existence of the gardener—God—is neither verifiable nor deniable; in the real world, the two beliefs have no meaning beyond that invested in them by their adherents. The question of God is moot, Jazz gloats. That's a powerful story, Blaine agrees, disingenuously. Powerful?! Jazz replies. It's *conclusive*. Oh yeah? But Blaine doesn't let on a thing when the windstorm abates at this very instant.

As I worked on the eventually discarded scene at the airfield and the modified Transfiguration scene and the ride with the Christian bikers, as I worried about Joe S.'s remark that we have to crucify this messiah, too, in some way, Blaine starts thinking in these terms *in* the story. Again, what's his mission? What's his message? What's he got to preach about? He is a Suffering Servant, but God has already offered a means of redemption and salvation for those who feel this need. Stripped to its essence, the narrative argument in *Deity* has been quite simple—Is Blaine for real? Okay, but how does this divinity play *today*? Okay, so what should Blaine do?—and this progression reaches its inevitable climax at the Bellagio in Las Vegas, where he wins the hundred thousand dollars while the dealers and pit bosses remain clueless, and then takes the money to the homeless shelter. (Using a card-counting system at the blackjack tables won't work at the major casinos over the long run, because your resulting bets will have a telltale pattern that gives you away, if only after the fact when the managers review the eye-in-the-sky tapes. However, if you, like Blaine, can stand pat on twelve with the dealer showing royalty, or hit on seventeen with the dealer showing a four, and win hand after hand with such crazy play, you're home free, because there's no accounting for your success.) Blaine could explode the logic of John Wisdom's parable in a million ways, but now, in Las Vegas, of all places, he knows that he won't do so. He'll play Robin Hood, but he won't play God.

But then why is Blaine here at all? Here's one plausible answer to that popular book-club question: while Jesus Christ was dispatched to provide us with a means of redemption, because those were the terms in which God viewed Himself and us at the time, maybe now He really is having second thoughts, and maybe these thoughts are reflected in and then reinforced by the ambivalence of this new incarnation. Maybe there's something to process theology after all: maybe Blaine is the deity of the Invisible Church of the Anonymous Christians.

Sartre would know what I'm talking about here. Remember that conversation between him and de Beauvoir in the beginning of this afterword, in which the old atheist can't shake his contradictory feeling that he's a being who could come only from a creator? That's not the end of the story, because de Beauvoir then asks Sartre what has been the benefit of nevertheless not believing in God, of having lived a life apart from Him? I want to quote Sartre's reply: "It has strengthened my freedom and made it sounder. At the present time this freedom is not there to give God what he asks for; it is there for the discovery of myself and to give me what I ask of myself. That's essential. And then my relations with others are direct: they no longer pass through the intermediary of the Omnipotent; I don't need God in order to love my neighbor. . . . This life owes nothing to God; it was what I wanted it to be. . . . And when now I reflect upon it, it satisfies me; and I do not need to pass by God for that."

Blaine might raise his glass here. Certainly he'd understand the sentiment. In any event, he now knows that there's not going to be a grand coming-out party for him after all—not quietly, not dramatically, not implicitly, not explicitly, not de facto, not de jure, not from the grave, not from the sky, not with a sword, not with a plowshare, not on a white horse, not on a black horse, not at high noon, not at midnight, not today, not tomorrow—or maybe tomorrow, because who knows about tomorrow, but for the second time in two thousand years, we have dismissed a messiah with our disbelief. Or we could put a more positive spin on the situation: the time is not yet ripe. God hasn't given up on us yet. We've made some progress in certain areas; we have some more time to straighten things out. Either way, this new incarnation, like the ghostly neutrino, will come and go without anyone's taking its measure. Blaine's main chance turns out to be the exploitation of a deck of playing cards for the benefit of the poor. Yes, he feels some responsibility for believers of all faiths, but the fate of the planet will nevertheless remain on hold for now; exeunt Blaine and his divine purposes.

But exeunt how? The devil was definitely in this detail. You can imagine the number of eventual endings I tried, at least a dozen. (The Gospel writers had it easy by comparison, if I do say so. They differ in the details they choose to relate—for example, Matthew is the only one who mentions the earthquake that accompanies Jesus's death on the cross, the broken tombs, the risen saints who go forth into the city and appear to many—but the basic ending was a given for all of them. Mine wasn't.) In one early discard, the scaffolding outside Father Harris's rectory collapses, and kills Blaine, not Harris himself. But Blaine can't die such a death.

Nor can he commit suicide. We don't think of Jesus's decisions prior to the Crucifixion as in any way suicidal, but from the stern secular perspective, his was a willful death. I thought I had to find out where this might lead with Blaine and intended to try a few sketches in this direction, but the idea made me too uncomfortable, and I set it aside instanter. Plus Blaine, unlike Jesus, has a wife and a young son. He may be a bit of a rogue male, but he's not an irresponsible cad. He's not going to leave them bereft.

I tried switching the order between the road trip out West and the journey to the Holy Land so that the story could end at the Sea of Galilee, where Blaine *does* choose a certain dramatic public demonstration straight out of Scripture in which water plays a major role. Another, closely related ending gave a whole new meaning to the adage about the good guy who walks off into the sunset: what if Blaine decides to do exactly this, while standing on the beach in Santa Monica? Walking the waters of the world in the cause of peace is a wonderful image, so wonderful that I gave some thought to recasting the whole story so it could end this way, but it just wasn't right. I'd never thought of *Deity* as a fairy tale. And even if Blaine had embarked on this crusade, we still wouldn't have peace, would we? That seems beyond the merely miraculous.

Yet another rejected conclusion finds Blaine

pausing at the fence line of a cemetery—
specifically, the vest-pocket Jewish abode right
across the street from the Barnes & Noble on
Twenty-first Street—on a rainy fall afternoon
when his future and the world's are as cloudy
as the skies. Is he finally going to raise the
dead? He really wants to, but he knows it
would prove nothing he doesn't already know
and cause problems that no one needs, so he
turns for the bookstore instead. Or what if
Blaine changes form, in the godlike way of the
classical deities? No, because I consider him
bound by the strictures of monotheism, not
those of the pantheon, and it's not at all clear
that Jesus Christ himself could have changed
form, even had he wanted to. Like us, deities
are endowed with inherent natures, and deep
reasons argue against such powers of transformation for any Judeo-Christian incarnation.

Then I worked with the story of Sabbatai
Sevi, the seventeenth-century Jew who lived in
Constantinople and became the object of the

largest messianic movement in Judaic history. In the end, the Muslim clerics of Constantinople gave this claimant the choice of proving his status as the Jewish messiah by stopping a flight of arrows with only his skin for armor, or renouncing his faith and converting to Islam. The idea of being the messiah hadn't been Sevi's to begin with—it was foisted on him by his prophet, Nathan of Gaza, possessed of a mystical vision—so this was a relatively easy call. The erstwhile messiah chose apostasy, and that was the end of that. Perhaps Blaine could be similarly challenged, with similar results? No, because he's not a false messiah.

I'll contend that all of those rejects have intriguing qualities, but the most radical of the unused conclusions was the one in which *Deity* switches midparagraph from a third- to a first-person narration, with the narrator astonishing the reader with the revelation that *he* is Blaine, that Blaine isn't a fictional character, that the novel isn't really a novel at all. It's an autobiography, almost a trial balloon: this is happening, folks, *I am here,* but I've decided to lie low for now, and because of all the publicity that will accompany the publication of this sensational new gospel, I've just acquired a new identity with the help of some bleach, fake bushy eyebrows, and a beard. "For the foreseeable future," that discarded draft concluded, "your Savior will abide anonymously among His people as a common man (of some means now) whose wife (with whom I'm no longer living, as you know) is expecting our second child (a daughter). Check all future editions of *The Deity Next Door* to find out where things stand."

Reading that one, my agent and editor were nonplussed, my wife more so, and all my other test readers also condemned this outcome as way too tricky, too O. Henry–esque in the extreme. They said it burst the bubble of believability about Blaine that I'd worked so hard to sustain, because an author claiming to be divine is not divine, prima facie, but only out of his mind. Why?! Why would readers accept Blaine's divinity on the author's say-so but not the author's *own* divinity on his own say-so? What's the difference? Didn't Jesus Christ declare his own divinity in just this manner? He did,[*] but I ended up agreeing that readers would nevertheless recoil from such self-aggrandizement, even if fictional, on the narrator's part.

But what happens instead? I still had no idea how to usher Blaine offstage. I only had him back in the city from out West, sunburned, exhausted, but enlightened in his apartment on Twenty-fourth Street; alone, since Melanie and Tim now live in Minneapolis, following her transfer; and back at work solving those otherwise intractable programming problems. Across the way, the pregnant woman has delivered her beautiful little daughter, Isis. The struggling writer has landed a coveted assignment from

---

[*]Matthew 28:18; John 8:58; etc.

the *New Yorker*. (I had one of those. Good luck.)
The lonely woman and the lonely man have
started dating—a pat development, for sure,
but I can't help that; it happened. John Riley's
widow and her young son have returned to their
apartment, and she takes over the boy's chess
lessons, and he's doing well enough without his
father, it seems. So for some of his neighbors, at
least, things are looking up as Blaine looks on—
and here was my answer, right in front of me.

All along, I'd been confident that Christian
readers would accept my implicit premise that
deity would be a whole different thing today
without feeling that I'm necessarily implying
that deity two thousand years ago was also a
whole different thing than advertised; likewise,
I thought the secular audience might go along
with the story of the new messiah without bringing charges against my sanity, because, let's
face it, there is something intriguing about the
idea. In short, I thought (correctly) that both
parties would be grown-up about the story as a

whole, and I finally convinced myself that everyone would also be grown-up about a conclusion sans fireworks. The idea that the messiah will come riding down on a cloud next time won't work today, but the idea that he lives among us—again—but with his divine mission publicly undeclared and therefore unresolved—well, I guess the success of the novel confirms that you find this vision at least as plausible as, and definitely more palatable than, the one in Revelation. I know I do. And to those readers of early drafts who insisted I needed a big ending, even if Blaine doesn't take over the world, I said and still say that this is a big ending—not a bang, but not a whimper, either—because how often has a deity just stepped aside, if only for the moment? To my knowledge—and, more convincingly, to my man Paul P.'s knowledge—never in the history of literature. (And to those who accused me of just setting things up for a sequel—well, the nerve.)

All along, I'd put the emphasis on Blaine's

humanity, not on his deity. In this incarnation, too, God has become human and the human has become God. It's Blaine's *humanity* that really grows, so it's from this humanity that his deity learns and therefore grows. For the time being, it seemed to me, his future would be of a man, not of a god, and once I had it, I never wavered from that concluding scene with Blaine back in his place in the big city, his hands behind his head, his feet on the desk, his beloved Gore-Tex at his side (a detail I omitted from the novel, for some wrong reason), his passion still profound as our apartmentalized lives unfold before him, but with his future—personal as well as cosmic—still on hold.

There you have it. I think I've answered all of your more important questions except the one I've been asked more times than I care to count, what I "really believe." That's always the phrase, and many readers have apparently concluded that I'm a sly nonbeliever playing the devil's advocate, while others suspect that I'm an even slier evangelical Christian playing a different devil's advocate. (Only with this publishing experience have I truly understood that a writer concocts a different story for every reader.) For months after the book came out I stumbled through assorted uninteresting agnostic answers until one frigid night in a bookstore in Des Moines. "What do I really believe?" I repeated to the crowd of thirty or so, and I laughed as I replied, "Well, I guess you could call me an inerrantist, because I believe every word of *The Deity Next Door.*"

June 2002
Puako, The Big Island, Hawaii

ACKNOWLEDGMENTS

A host of early readers helped me with this story. I thank Steve Gaskins, Andy and Louis Grigar, Steve Hanks, Joe Kane, Doug Magee, Desiree Pilachowski, Gaines Post, Judy Ryser, Steve Salinger, Dick Symonds, John Thornton, and Bonnie and Fred Waitzkin. Four friends— Gary Fisketjon, Eva Freund, Jim Parker, and Paul Pines—went way beyond the call of friendship, critiquing multiple drafts and making multiple key suggestions. And my wife Patty went even further, of course, reading every draft and entertaining every issue.

A special thanks to Wayne Grier, the inerrantist himself, and Luis Pantoja.

I wrote the second draft of this book—the one that got me over the hump—at the wonderful Taos-area home of the aforementioned Steve Hanks and his wife Sheree Livney. I don't imagine it would have happened anywhere else.

I owe just about everything regarding *The Afterword* to my agent, Joe Spieler, and my editor, Edward Kastenmeier. When it was a 6,000-word story, Joe said, Keep going. When it was 15,000 words, Edward chimed in. They've stuck by it ever since; they've worked on it about as hard as I have.

Finally, ultimate gratitude to everyone at Pantheon. They really publish their books.

ABOUT THE AUTHOR

Mike Bryan lives in London Terrace Gardens in New York City.

This book was set in De Vinne, a modern typeface. The modern faces are sharply drawn with an almost mathematical exactness and are designed for use on hard, smooth-surfaced papers, in contrast to the oldstyle faces, which are more freely drawn and were originally designed for use on softer handmade sheets. De Vinne, alone among the moderns, has a most interesting character when used on antique papers, as it frequently is.

The modern types were first made about 1790. Soon immensely popular, they became grossly distorted, each typefounder trying to outdo his competitors by exaggerating the modern characteristics. It was not until late in the nineteenth century that the modern type regained its original sanity of design, largely through the influence of the great American printer Theodore Low De Vinne, in whose honor this typeface was named.